LAST OF THE GULLIVERS

PHILOMEL BOOKS

A division of Penguin Young Readers Group. Published by The Penguin Group.
Penguin Group (USA) Inc., 375 Hudson Street, New York, NY 10014, U.S.A. Penguin
Group (Canada), 90 Eglinton Avenue East, Suite 700, Toronto, Ontario M4P 2Y3, Canada
(a division of Pearson Penguin Canada Inc.). Penguin Books Ltd, 80 Strand, London
WC2R 0RL, England. Penguin Ireland, 25 St. Stephen's Green, Dublin 2, Ireland
(a division of Penguin Books Ltd). Penguin Group (Australia), 250 Camberwell Road,
Camberwell, Victoria 3124, Australia (a division of Pearson Australia Group Pty Ltd).
Penguin Books India Pvt Ltd, 11 Community Centre, Panchsheel Park, New Delhi -
110 017, India. Penguin Group (NZ), 67 Apollo Drive, Rosedale, Auckland 0632,
New Zealand (a division of Pearson New Zealand Ltd). Penguin Books (South Africa)
(Pty) Ltd, 24 Sturdee Avenue, Rosebank, Johannesburg 2196, South Africa.
Penguin Books Ltd, Registered Offices: 80 Strand, London WC2R 0RL, England.

Published simultaneously in Canada. Printed in the United States of America.
Edited by Tamra Tuller. Design by Amy Wu. Text set in 12-point Berkeley.

Library of Congress Cataloging-in-Publication Data
Crocker, Carter. Last of the Gullivers / Carter Crocker. p. cm.
Summary: After orphaned twelve-year-old Michael Pine, who seems headed for trouble,
meets old Lem Gulliver, he finds new purpose as protector of the Lilliputians who live
in Lem's back garden, even if that means saving them from one another. [1. Conduct
of life—Fiction. 2. Adventure and adventurers—Fiction. 3. Size—Fiction. 4. Gangs—
Fiction. 5. Orphans—Fiction.] I. Swift, Jonathan, 1667–1745. Gulliver's travels.
II. Title. PZ7.C86968Las 2012 [Fic]—dc22 2011003676

ISBN 978-0-399-24231-1
10 9 8 7 6 5 4 3 2 1

LAST OF THE GULLIVERS

CARTER CROCKER

PHILOMEL BOOKS | An Imprint of Penguin Group (USA) Inc.

*For Ms. Brown's class,
among others*

♦ ♦ ♦

ACKNOWLEDGMENTS
With thanks to Tamra Tuller
and Kiffin Steurer
for their guidance and encouragement

FROM THE DIARY OF YOUNG
FRIGARY TIDDLIN

Mid-September—

We were only children when this journey began, back in a time and a place I can't even remember. We have sailed many seas since then, and weathered many storms. We've spent endless weeks in windless water, been without compass, lost & drifting.

But now, we have found what we were seeking: the Blessed Isle lies before us. The People there send a dozen boats to guide our tired & tattered ship to harbor. They line the waterfront, we at the rail, each side silent & unsure.

It is our Grand Panjandrum who speaks—

"Citizens, Friends, Brothers, Sisters, we have returned!" he bellows, with a voice full of pride & thunder.

And he is answered by loud nothing. Oh, the looks on their faces! What is it, curiosity, fear?

"We've been to a world beyond dreaming," he goes on, "and seen sights impossible to imagine. We have lived among a race of Giants, battled bloodthirsty monsters & faced unknowable peril. Ours is a story of wonder & woe, of courage & cowardice, of longing & love."

But there is only more silence. They must think we've gone mad from the voyage . . .

PART ONE

◆

SAILING AGAINST THE WIND

CHAPTER ONE

———— ✦ ————

THE VILLAGE OF LIES AND MIRACLES

One year before—

When he was young, Michael didn't believe in magic or ghosts or dreams. He didn't believe that a race of Little Folk wandered the clover fields. He didn't believe in anything, really. He wasn't curious or adventurous, impulsive or impatient, the way children are meant to be.

Michael Pine was twelve years old, today, and small for that age. He had the broad open face of the country, wary blue eyes and hair that wouldn't comb. He lived in a small flat with his Uncle Freddie, who was yelling at him: "Ah, crud. You better not be late again!"

"Didn't know you cared so much about my education," the boy mumbled back.

"I care if that school sends somebody to hassle me. Go on, go!"

Michael got his books and left. He headed up the wind-washed street and across a bridge on the dry River Stone. He went through the Market Square and past St. Edwards, the town half-hid from him in the cold rain, streetlights only a blush on the mist. Ahead, his schoolhouse rose from a hill and the bell was ringing even now.

They were studying House Sparrows that day and, when the rain let up, the teacher took them to the schoolyard to look for little birds. "All right, who can—Jimmy, don't put that in your mouth—who can tell me something about sparrows?" Hetty Bellknap asked over the shrill wind.

Michael hid from her view, behind a classmate. It was a skill he'd spent a lifetime on, fading away like this.

"Ms. Bellknap, Ms. Bellknap," this from Penelope Rees Jones, *always* Penelope Rees.

"Yes, dear?"

"House Sparrows are tiny, delicate things," said Penelope.

"Good, anything else?"

"They have small families," again Penelope Rees, who left no question unanswered and whose own house held a flock of uncles, aunts, cousins, others.

"Females usually lay three to six eggs," said Hetty. "What about predators?"

"Weasels and Sparrow Hawks try to kill them and eat them," Penelope Rees told the class.

"And ducks, too." This from Charlie Ford, the policeman's son. "I bet a good-sized duck could kill one, easy." Charlie always had answers, never right ones, and a nose that wouldn't stop dripping.

"Well, maybe, Charles, but ducks tend to feed around water."

"Owls and people can hurt them," Penelope Rees explained.

"That's true, Penelope. The House Sparrows are very vulnerable."

"I was going to say that, Ms. Bellknap," piped Penelope. "They're tiny and delicate and very vulnerable."

"But vulnerable creatures get by, don't they?" the teacher went on. "They have ways of thriving despite the odds against them." She sent the children around the yard to look for little birds and Michael wandered to the back fence.

"Over here, eejit." It was Robby and Peter and the rest of the Boys, calling from the other side.

"Let's go, squire," said Peter. "Nick's waitin'."

"Can't," Michael told them. "Can't ditch school again. I'd get detention, I guess, maybe exclusion."

"You'll get worse, you don't c'mon," Robby told him back.

"Let's move it, Mike," this from Gordy. "Don't want to get Nick in a bad mood."

Michael saw Ms. Bellknap with a noisy gaggle of students: Penelope Rees had found a sparrow's nest under the eaves. Charlie was a few feet away, by a tree, watching Michael. Charlie was always somewhere near. He had trouble making friends and keeping friends and that runny nose didn't help.

"You didn't see me go, Charlie. You don't say anything to anybody, right, or we'll both get in trouble. You understand?"

"Hey, I'm not *that* stupid."

"If you say," said Michael. "Go on, now, go back with the rest of 'em." Michael jumped the fence and followed his Boys into the heart of the village.

Moss-on-Stone was here when the Romans came, back when a river still flowed the valley. The People learned to make wool and the wool made them rich. With the sun-colored rocks that were everywhere, they built a golden city and called it *Moss-on-Stone, Where the Wind's Always Blown.*

And there was wind, always. In summer, it blew too hot; in winter, too cold; day and night, it never stopped. This was a lively place once, busy with fairs and festivals. On Market Day, Shepherds brought their herds down Sheep

Street, a lane built to funnel the flocks: the street began at full width and narrowed to two and a half feet, so the sheep could be counted as they squeezed through.

In the old days, there was music here, all kinds. It came from street bands, out of pub windows, from old bankers and tired farmers. Everyone in the village made music and people came from miles to hear it.

Back then the world was full of magic and mystery. It was a superstitious time and these folk scratched marks on their fireplaces to scare off witches, had tonics for all ailments, found omens everywhere. They thought a stork nesting on the roof was good luck and they knew for fact that a lost race of Little Folk wandered the clover fields.

But that was long ago. Now the wool is made in other places, the fairs don't happen, and the storks are gone. And only the crazy ones see Little Folk in the clover.

And listen close. Hear it? These days, there's no music. Only wind and always wind. These days, they'll tell you that the beautiful adventures have been had and there are no grand journeys left to take.

But of course they are wrong.

"It's your time, Michael," said Nick. "Today's the first day of the rest of your life. Today's the day you get to be one of us." Nick Bottoms was sixteen, leader of the gang, a handsome boy with a good-looking Mom and Dad and all of them useless liars.

"Big day, squire." "Mikey's growing up on us." Gordy and Peter and Phil and Robby were the rest of Nick's Boys and they were gathered in an alley off Grub Street.

If you'd asked him, Michael couldn't have told you why he joined this gang. Maybe they were family to him, uncles, nephews, cousins, that big boisterous family he never had. Or maybe they gave some direction to his drifting life.

Just in the door at Tiswas Electric, high-tech toys were stacked in towering display and, at the top, the last glorious Game Machine in the city, maybe the world. "Go for it," Nick told him.

"Nah, Nick," said Michael, a whisper. "I'm not ready."

"What're you, almost ten? You got to start somewhere."

"Let somebody else do it," said Michael. "And I'm twelve."

"Like I said. It's your *time*." The way Nick saw things, this was a rite, a passage, a crossroads everybody had to reach. "It's nothing once you're used to it," and he pushed the boy on.

Michael stumbled across the street and tripped past the bookshop run by the two Mrs. Daniels, Esther and Stella.

"What are you doing here, Michael. Isn't there school," from Esther.

"And Freddie," from Stella, "has he found a job yet."

These weren't questions, but the boy answered: "No school, no job."

He moved on by the secondhand shop, called *Gadbury's* because a Gadbury always owned it. Junk from the store streamed out the door and onto the pavement: an old clock, a plow, chairs, a red bike, magazines, last week's high-tech toys, all else.

And half-buried in the front window, a model ship that had been there longer than anybody could remember. It was big as a sofa, had three tall masts, sails furled, and rigging fine as a spider's web. A tiny tattered flag hung from a spar and under that, a figurehead: a lively little mermaid with billows of red-yellow hair and green eyes set firmly on the future. The model wasn't in good shape, a mast broken, held with tape, and dust over the whole thing. *Adventure*, she was called.

"Move it, eejit!" came a yell from the alley, across the street. "Before Christmas, eh?" "This ain't gonna feed the baby!"

And Nick's voice: "Remember—this is your *time*."

Maybe it was. Michael had reached a crossroads and had to make a choice. The boy bit his lip and ran into the store and grabbed the high holy Game Machine, and the rest of the stack came timbering down in an endless crash. He backed out the door and into the street and in front of a large dark car. Brakes screamed and tire rubber burned and the car slid across the shimmering pavement, right into Michael. He fell to the road with a hard hollow thump.

Nick's Boys didn't move, but froze where they were.

"Stone me," one of them finally said. "Nailed him good." "The dumb squit." "Is he dead?"

Even Michael wasn't sure of the answer to that question.

He smelled the sour rubber and felt the car's heat and heard the blood coursing in his head. He was still alive, lying flat in the street, holding the Game Machine, safe, secure. "Told him I wasn't ready," Michael grumbled to himself.

Then there was shouting from every side. Tiswas ran out of his store, cursing, screaming. Frances Froth, the small and excitable woman from the pet shop down the block, was hopping around like a little caged dog. Gadbury hurried from Gadbury's and tripped on a red bike and fell to his knees with a grunt. Esther and Stella peered from their little bookshop.

When Michael got to his feet, he saw a young girl in the car's backseat. She was his age, he thought, strawberry blond, green-eyed, a fine band of freckles across her nose.

"Well, that must've hurt," she said.

"I'm fine, I guess," Michael told her.

He saw her bloodred blazer, the uniform of St. Brendan's. He saw how she watched him, with a wide wondering look.

"Crazy yahoo!" the driver was shouting.

"Lousy. Cheap. Thieving. Punk!" This was Mr. Tiswas and his cigarette-ruined voice.

"Get him get him get him!" Frances Froth squeaked, squealed, tiny and overwrought like a hamster in a wheel.

And from over in the alley, a last voice, Nick's voice: *"You flat-out fool!"*

There was a big cop galloping at him and the green-eyed girl leaned from the car to ask, "Well? What happens now?"

CHAPTER TWO

———— ◆ ————

IN A FIELD OF CLOVER

Michael dropped the Game Machine in the street and went running. The Boys were gone from the alley and he ran alone down the closing-in Sheep Street and on through the Market Square and past St. Edwards. There was a siren now, and another, another, louder, louder. He turned again, up an alley, and ran harder. He ran across Stow Street, every part of him aching. His breath burned inside him and he was too scared to think of stopping.

He passed the Inn, unlevel with the weight of years, and ran till the shops became houses and these became farms, the village fast-fading in the mist. He jumped a low wall and ripped his trousers on the sharp stone comb. He didn't know where he was or was going, but he kept on. He followed old tractor tracks through fields of wheat that traced the shape of a never-ending wind.

For a minute, he thought he heard music. But no, these were sirens, howling like a pack of wolves in the valley. Wolves, hungry for him. He ran until the sound and the wind were gone. He came to a meadow, where the air was still, but full of life. A badger ambled into the nettle, and Michael stopped to pull spiky cleavers from his socks.

A Jay was squawking at him from a tree branch. "You think you got problems," the boy told it. "I ditched school, robbed a store, got hit by a car, chased by cops—and it's not even lunchtime yet."

He saw, on the far side of the meadow, a small house—what was left of one—an old stone cottage, rough-walled, whitewashed, roof of thatch. In a better day, it would have been one of those fairy-tale places where tourists stop to take pictures.

But it was a sad sight now, forgotten and falling apart, small diamond windows broken and stuffed with newspaper. By the sagging, uncertain chimney there was a large and empty bird's nest. The rock wall around the front was mostly fallen in, the walk gone to weed.

The place looked unlived in, unlivable. And, to a twelve year old felon, it looked like a good place to hide for a while.

Michael tried the door, but it was locked or swollen shut. He went to the back of the house and saw a stone wall around the garden, a huge wall, ten feet tall and mossed over. He walked and found no door, no gate, no way in or way out.

Then he heard the music, coming from the other side. It was very strange music, like none he'd ever heard, peaceful, wild, sad, happy, and all at once, if that was possible.

And then it was gone.

He went on around the back garden, walking the length of the long ambling wall, until he came to the cottage again. He found a low window, unlocked, and wrestled it up a few inches. That was enough. They say a rat can fit through a hole the size of a fifty cent piece, and Michael squeezed through this narrow slot and was in the cold dark kitchen. He stopped and listened and heard no one. He moved on and found a door to the back garden. It was open, a crack, moonlight fanning across the floor. He stepped through it and into a small courtyard full of clover, with overgrown shrubs hiding the rest of the garden.

The music must have come from back there, somewhere farther. Michael was about to start down the walkway when a gunshot tore through the windless air. The boy fell, head-first, to the brick path and rolled into the clover.

This, he was thinking, as everything went dark, *just isn't my day.*

When he woke up again—was it minutes, hours, days?—there was a moon and there was blood. His head had been bleeding, a lot, but wasn't now. He tried to sit up and couldn't. There were small fuzzy spots of light around him. Was this the will-o'-the-wisp that Freddie and his mates sometimes talked about? A superstition said the lights were the lost, wandering souls of the un-baptized, unsure how to get to Heaven, not meant for Hell. Michael lay there and moaned and the little lights went scattering in every direction, into the untended shrubs.

He tried to sit up, but was lashed to the ground, held in some spidery web. Fine binding twine crisscrossed his chest, arms, legs, everywhere. He felt something crawl onto him and over him and he tried to see, but his head and neck were bound, too.

He yelled out—"Shoo, go away!"—and whatever-it-was hurried into the dark. He heard a sound like words, a muddy murmur from the shadows of the clover. The boy had never been as scared as this and could hardly breathe from it.

Before he found a voice to scream with, a mountainous dog was on him, its hot slaver pouring into his face.

"All right, Whitby," came a voice, "settle now," and the dog settled but didn't seem happy about it. "No, no," the voice was saying. "He's not dead."

Michael lay still, eyes shut.

"They thought you were a bear."

He opened his eyes and saw a shape against the moon, a man, tall and bent and old as dirt, wild white hair, a beard glowing with starlight. The man used a walking stick to break the threads and Michael leapt to his feet and went running.

He ran through the house and out the front door, ran the many long miles to the village, and straight into the big arms of a policeman. He was put in the back of a dim reeking van and wind whistled at the wire grate. A crowd pushed close to see.

"Is that the boy?" Stanley Ford, the policeman, asked.

"S'him," grunted Tiswas.

The dark-car man was there, too. "That's the one, that's the yahoo."

"It's him it's him it's him!" said the tiny pet shop woman, Francis Froth, excited and hopping about.

Gadbury nodded.

And the cop asked, "What's your name, boy?"

"Michael."

"Michael what?"

"Pine."

"Your head hurt?"

"Not too bad."

"What happened to you, Michael Pine?"

"I. Guess. I. Fell."

"How old are you?" asked Stanley, tall fellow, decent and patient and often lonely.

"Twelve. Twelve today."

The officer sighed and said, "Now, Michael, is this any way to spend your birthday?"

CHAPTER THREE

PIG'S NOSE, PARSLEY & ONION SAUCE

The wind of Moss-on-Stone was maddening and ever-there. It uncombed your hair, grabbed papers from your hands, and whistled through every unseen crack in your house. On the afternoon Michael went to Youth Court, the wind was very wet and very cold.

The court buildings sat at the north edge of the town, grim places with stained concrete walls and murky windows. Nick's Boys were across in a car park, watching, waiting.

"That little eejit's going to rat on us." Robby was oldest and meanest and he hated Michael. "The little eejit's going to rat us out, you watch, you'll see."

"Y'really think?" asked Gordy. "Y'think, really?" Gordy was as big as a Gloucester pig and half as smart.

Phil, a quiet boy who had running dreams like dogs, said nothing.

"Now here's the way I see it." It was Peter, the one who thought *everything* through. "They'll let squire off easy. He's littlest and youngest and they go easy on young little ones. He's, what, ten? They'll go easy on him."

"Y'think, really?" Gordy again. "Y'really think?"

They'd all been locked up in YOI, the Young Offenders Institution at Ambridge, one time or another. Robby had been in six times. Nick alone had kept out.

"Michael's smarter than you lot put together," said Nick. "He knows what's expected of him."

The building was as plain inside as out and smelled like ink and sweat. There were a few brown chairs in the back and these were for onlookers, but onlookers weren't let in the Youth Court. There were four bent military desks set in a square, for the Court Usher, the Clerk, and the Magistrates.

Michael sat, quiet, unsure and ashamed.

Freddie shifted, edgy and uneasy: he'd been here too many times when he was younger. Michael's duty solicitor, Mr. Fenworth, was there and silent, too. He was a tall and reclusive man who had no children and didn't think much of them.

The Court Clerk came in first: Maxine Bellknap, an intent woman with a gardener's rosy glow. She had been a barrister here once, a good one, had retired many times, but never found the heart to leave the Court. Her daughter Hetty was Michael's teacher.

Mr. Tiswas sat in a chair to the side, alone, staring at the floor. Stanley Ford, the policeman, was in the next row.

Three Magistrates entered. The Chief Magistrate, Horace Ackerby II, was a giant and weighed a hundred pounds too many. He had cat eyes, a mop of messy hair, and the fiercest, shortest temper in Moss-on-Stone. Once a bank official, he'd become a Magistrate late in life. The other two looked like old children.

"The first duty of man," Ackerby finally said, "is the seeking after of truth. It was Cicero said that, not me. But it's what I'm after. Truth is what I seek. Tell me, child—the Truth—did you steal the, ah, the, um"—he checked his notes—"the Game Machine?"

Michael sat, silent, uncertain.

The lawyer Fenworth said, "*Answerrr.*"

And Michael answered, "No."

Fenworth sighed, "The *truuuth.*"

And Michael said, "No, sir, but I tried."

"The child spends his day how?" the Magistrate asked, but didn't wait for an answer. "Drifting, yes, looking for trouble? The parents are where?"

"Dead, Horace, car crash," Freddie answered, helpful. "I'm stuck with him now."

"I believe you're paid a stipend by the government," said one of the other Magistrates.

"Not much of one, I'm not," Freddie grunted back.

"He's never been arrested," Fenworth offered.

"Or never been caught." Ackerby took off his glasses and rubbed his eyes and said, "I wonder, child, what are your dreams?"

Michael didn't know what to say and said nothing.

"Tell me what—beyond stealing—are the things that interest you? That excite your blood?"

The boy could only shrug.

The Chief Magistrate put his glasses back on and raked a hand through his wild hair. "If you were as old as I am— and, yes, I'm old—you'd know that we chart a course for our lives, choosing right paths and wrong ones. Is there a reason, at your young age, you've chosen this?"

And again, Michael had no answer.

"The course to prison? Will you go where the wind blows you, boy—nowhere else?" Ackerby hit the old steel desk with a huge hammy fist. He was a banshee now in a spittle-spewing fury. The other Magistrates shifted in their small cold chairs. "Do you want to end up *like him*?!" He meant Freddie. "Is that the best you can dream!?"

"Ah, c'mon now, Horace," from Freddie.

"You keep company with thugs, you'll amount to *nothing*! You hear me?!"

Fenworth quietly whined, *"Answerrr."*

"Yes," said Michael. "Yes, sir," he added, "I hear you."

The Chief Magistrate grew just as quickly calm. He looked past Michael, to the Court Clerk and some unspoken words passed between them. "We are proposing an Action Plan Order. The boy will be given an after-school job and will work two hours each day. He will no longer consort with gang members. Each weekday, for twelve months, he will check in with an officer at six thirty in the evening. He will meet weekly to review his progress with Ms. Bellknap."

"And who's s'posed to haul him all the way over"—Freddie saw Ackerby's cold eyes—"that'd be me, wouldn't it?"

"Ms. Bellknap will prepare a report," the Magistrate went on, "for myself and the others. Is this all clear to you?"

Michael nodded, it was clear.

"Have you anything to say for yourself?"

"No. No, sir. Nothing."

"Ms. Bellknap will fill you in on the particulars." The men stood, three at once, and Horace Ackerby turned back to Michael. "There are better courses a life can take. Surprise us, eh? See what else you can find."

Michael only nodded and Freddie only grumbled, "Ah, crud."

The boy never knew how close he'd come to YOI. The Chief Magistrate was sick of thugs who stole from the people, their Game Machines and peace of mind. He wanted to make an example of Michael and show that *he*, Horace Ackerby, JP, could put a stop to this kind of thing.

It was the Court Clerk, Maxine Bellknap, who saved Michael. Her daughter Hetty was his teacher and she knew there was still hope for the boy: she had seen a light in him, a spark that still flickered. "The Court gives you leeway in these juvenile cases," Maxine had told Ackerby.

"That's right, Ms. Bellknap. It does." The Magistrate was a man who liked routine and leeway bothered him.

"It isn't my place to say, but I was thinking—well, of a deferment. A deferment of sentence. Make the boy work and repay the loss to Mr. Tiswas."

"He's too young," Ackerby grunted. "What is he, ten?"

"Twelve," Maxine told him. "Young, but just old enough that a job might steer him away from bad influences."

"It'd let him off very easy, too," Ackerby moaned. "I can give him a harsher sentence than that."

"Of course you can. But I was thinking. Maybe it's structure he needs. Something to give reason to his life. If he had a job. I was thinking, you could draft an agreement with the boy. A contract. He'd sign it and if he missed work or caused trouble—well, then," said Maxine, making it up as she went.

"That isn't a standard sentence," Ackerby said.

"No," Maxine admitted, "it isn't. But you could give him penalty points for every infraction. Like a Driving License. And if he lost too many points . . . well, then."

"Straight to YOI," the Magistrate said, chewing it over.

Maxine nodded. "To YOI."

"M'hm. I would call it a Liberty License."

"Well, then."

That evening, as they headed back to the flat, rain fell in a cold wind and Freddie mumbled, "Isn't fair. Have a life of my own. Now I got to take you to court every week. *Cruuuuud.*"

At this same time, a short mile away, Chief Magistrate Horace Ackerby II took his usual table at the pub called *Folk-in-the-Clover,* by the fire, looking out on the windy and ghostless churchyard. He waited for Bertram, the wiry little cook, to bring him a meal of pig's nose with parsley-and-onion sauce, sautéed red cabbage, two pints of ale. When the tower bell rang seven, the Chief Magistrate, whose own children were grown and whose wife had died, began to eat alone.

He thought about the boy and wondered if the scheme would work. When Horace Ackerby had first seen Michael Pine, he'd seen himself as a child. They both had hair that wouldn't comb, and something else: the light inside, the flickering spark. Maybe, the Magistrate thought, Michael wasn't so far gone that a rescue couldn't be made. Perhaps if they got to him soon enough, while the light still burned . . .

Or was he wrong? Was he going too easy on the boy? There was a feeling in the country that all effort to reform young criminals had failed. Voices were rising and saying these thugs needed to learn that actions have consequences.

Maxine had better be right, Horace thought. If something went wrong, if Michael Pine went wrong, this would come back to haunt him worse than any graveyard ghost. The voices would rise against him and he'd be out of a job. *That* would be the consequence of his action. And being Chief Magistrate meant a lot to Horace Ackerby.

Words began to come to him and he spoke them, quietly, to himself . . .

THE ACKERBY LIBERTY LICENSE
A FIRST CASE STUDY
by H. Ackerby, JP

Michael Pine was a boy without dreams, a distrustful and uncurious lad who believed in nothing. He was drifting into crime, and worse lay ahead. Could I, Horace Ackerby II, Justice of the Peace, Chief Magistrate for Moss-on-Stone, change the course of this one young life?

CHAPTER FOUR

✦

THE EVER-SAME, NEVER-SAME SONG

They knew something had happened, but didn't know what. Their eyes were on him, wondering, all through the school day. The cut on his head was deep and should have been stitched, but Freddie said he'd have a scar and so what?

Ms. Bellknap said nothing and continued their studies. The class learned more about birds, endangered, exotic, extinct, even a mythological bird. The Phoenix, she told the class, was a magic creature that lived five hundred years and could heal suffering with a single teardrop. As its end grew near, the bird built a nest of myrrh and settled itself in and burst into flame. A new Phoenix rose from the ashes of the old.

"We find this myth all over the world," she told them. "In ancient Egypt, it was called the Bennu bird—a large heron, perhaps a stork—we can't be sure. There are versions in China, the Americas, the Middle East. Now you tell me—Jimmy, leave her alone—tell me what you think the story of the Phoenix means."

"Ms. Bellknap." Penelope Rees, as ever.

"Penelope?"

"It means sometimes things die and sometimes babies are born."

"Yes, Penelope Rees. It does mean that."

"What I think," Charlie Ford wiped his nose and said, "it's about tryin' again. It's like gettin' a second chance to get it right."

Ms. Bellknap thought for a moment. "Well, yes, Charles. It is that, isn't it?"

"Ms. Bellknap." Penelope once more.

"Yes, dear?"

"Michael is bleeding all over the place."

"Penelope Rees. Let's mind our own business."

The teacher gave Michael a tissue for his head and sent him to the school nurse. As the small and lavender-smelling woman cleaned the blood, he looked out the window and saw Nick's Boys waiting for him. They were gathered at the fence, like the stout sullen hawks he sometimes saw in the fields.

When school let out, they were still there, still waiting. But Michael never came. He'd been given a job at Fenn's Market and Hetty Bellknap drove him there as her mother, the Court Clerk, had asked.

The cramped little market was on a far edge of the village, on the road to Ambridge. "All right, come on," Mr. Fenn spat. He was a solid man, jowly and unmarried, and his words came in wet blasts. "I want every shelf— faced. That means tins, boxes, everything— facing out, lined up, straight across!"

Michael followed him through a storeroom, stacked floor to rafter with boxes, crates, bins, smelling like old vegetables. Fenn shoved a stubby thumb at an open shelf and told the boy to keep his schoolbooks here during work.

They moved down another narrow canyon. "Every day you make sure the shelves are full. Myron will— he'll show you how."

Myron was Fenn's teenaged nephew, friendless and fuzzy at the edges: it was hard to tell where Myron started and Myron stopped. He was usually in the back room, gnawing a peppermint stick. "Why— me?"

"Why not?" Fenn said as he left.

Myron told Michael what was expected of him and then he said, "Let's get one thing straight. I don't like you."

"You don't know me," said Michael.

"I don't have to know you to know I don't like you," Myron grunted and went back to eating peppermint.

Michael spent the next hours sweeping, stocking, cleaning, learning. As he worked, he quietly counted the minutes until he'd be free. It was almost five, closing time, when the door clanged open a last time.

The boy looked across the store as a man came in, tall, bent, silver-haired, old as earth. It might've been him, no, had to be him, from that night at the stone cottage.

"Codswallop," Fenn said to himself. "Crazy ol' loon. What's he doin' here?" Michael stood beside the grocer and watched the old man move slowly through the store. "Usually calls it in." Fenn waited by the counter. "Crazy— ol'— loon."

When the shopping was finally done, Fenn called for Michael to fill a canvas bag with a half-dozen tins of dog food, a bottle of Scotch whiskey, three cards of sewing needles, and a roll of fine twine.

"Mr. Fenn, do you carry rakes?"

"No, sir," Fenn coughed.

"I broke mine," the old man went on.

"Try down the road— DIY store."

"Happened the other night," the man was saying. "Heard a sound out back and what do you think I saw?"

Michael was sure the old man knew him and now he would tell Fenn.

"A bear."

Fenn spat out a total: "Thirty-four— twenty-two."

"Big as a Galloway cow. Charged right at me and I *whacked* him on the nose. Split my rake half in two. But he left me alone after that."

Fenn coughed. "There're no bears in Moss-on-Stone."

"Not anymore." The man paid Fenn. "I chased it off with a rake, didn't I?"

Fenn headed to the stockroom, but Michael stayed where he was and began to wonder, who *was* this old man?

"Come— here!" Fenn was yelling.

The old man started out and Michael said: "There aren't really bears."

"There are a lot of things that we never see," the man shrugged. "There are whole other worlds all around us, if we bother to look." He gave the boy a coin for a tip, a blackened old coin, probably worthless, and Michael put it deep in his pocket. "Not much to look at it," the man said. "But sometimes you have to look twice to see the value of a thing."

"Boy!" Fenn called again and he turned and the old man left.

Michael was walking down Sheep Street when he remembered the coin in his pocket. The clock at the Inn showed five fifteen and that left time to stop by the arcade in the back of the pub. He could try the coin in a video game: his favorite was the one called Cross-Country, steering a 2.4 liter V-8 Formula One over a digital landscape, the whole never-ending world blasting by on a screen.

He crossed the Market Square, where the fairs used to be, and was passing the rusty headstones of St. Edwards, when he heard the wind whistling. But no. It wasn't wind. It was someone whistling the tune he'd heard by the wall.

The boy hid in the yews by the refectory door, and watched and listened. Yes, it was that same tune: somber, silly, pointed and pointless. The doorknob turned behind him and hinges squealed and Father Drapier stepped out to lock the stone-sainted church. "Michael Pine? Haven't seen you in a while." Drapier looked and saw the old man headed up the road, out of town, whistling as he went. "Well. Haven't seen him in a while, either. Wonder what got him out of his house."

"Who is he?" asked Michael.

"Mr. Gulliver, who lives past the crossroads. Used to have a sister up there, but she's been gone for some time." The old priest was going over something in his head. "That man was ancient when I was a child. By now, he must be at least . . ." Father Drapier thought a moment more. "But, no. No. That couldn't possibly be right. Nobody's *that* old." And he wandered off, still adding it up.

Michael meant to go to the pub then, for the video game, but found himself following the fading song. He kept a distance as he trailed the old man out of the village and past spreading fields of clover.

The road narrowed to a single carriageway, where hogweed and bracken took back the crumbled pavement. He passed the ancient ruins of a church, a cow grazing in its nave, and he followed the old man to the crossroads.

Back in superstitious days, people thought this was a magic place: once the corpse of a witch was nailed to a stake here, to confuse her ghost so she'd never find the way back to haunt her executioners. People used to believe that kind of thing.

The man took the northwest road and Michael kept following. They moved through a forest where there might be bears and to the stone cottage where the old man disappeared in the stillness. The boy moved quietly to the back wall and heard the music again.

There was a half hour left till check-in at the Court and he sat against an ancient oak to listen. The song was lively now, and brooding, shimmering, soft, a memory, a lullaby.

And the boy tried to imagine: What other world lay beyond that wall?

———— ✦ ————

CHAPTER FIVE

INTO THE REMOTE NATION

I can tell you without any doubt," the tall man roared, "that in another five years, House Sparrows will be gone from this land. Just like the stork. They will be, so to speak, extinct."

"I imagine there must be some way to help the little things," Penelope said softly.

"I'm sure you imagine a lot of things," the man said, smiled. Ms. Bellknap had invited Dr. Emmanuel Kirleus, a bitter old professor, to talk to the students about endangered species. "House Sparrows used to feed on chickweed and dandelion, but we don't let these grow around our homes anymore. That's why the birds will die off."

"But what if," Penelope Rees again, even more quietly now, "what if I planted some seeds?"

"You ask too many questions, dear," Dr. Kirleus said, smiled. "This is science, not a fairy tale. You have to accept it. The birds will be gone in a few years, and forever."

Hetty squirmed, uneasy. She'd always taught her students that science was all about questions and the old professor's words bothered her. Still, on he droned and Michael could only hear the music, from beyond the wall, playing over and over in his head.

After school was done, he went to work at the little market. At six thirty, he checked in with a court officer, then went home to dinner and bed. This was the new rhythm of his life and he liked it. Mr. Fenn had been frightening at first, but really he was a lonely little man, ordinary and dull, and Michael liked that, too. If shelves were tidy, labels out, Fenn was no problem.

As the grocer began to trust the boy more, he gave him more to do. When Fenn saw that his whole store was organized and orderly, for the first time really, he decided to try Michael on the deliveries.

"Him—!?" Myron choked on a peppermint stick. "That's my job! I make the deliveries!"

"Yeah, and you keep foulin' it up, pig! Takin' scotch to the Daniels ladies, female things to a priest!"

"Well—" said Myron. "Well." Because Uncle Fenn was right. "But I— have a car. He's not even old enough to drive!"

"That— true? You can't drive?"

Michael nodded, it was true. "I'm twelve."

"Stop eating my peppermint!" Fenn shouted at Myron and turned to Michael. "You have a bicycle then."

"No," the boy answered. "No, sir."

"Codswallop!" Michael heard rats, or something like them, run across the rafters overhead. "There's one out back. Use it."

Fenn stalked out and Myron said: "Remember, boy. I—don't—like—you."

Mr. Fenn gave the boy a list, names, addresses, groceries, and the deliveries took him all across Moss-on-Stone, Where the Wind's Always Blown. Michael wore a blue vest and cap, and the groceries were balanced in baskets, one in front, two across the back, sometimes an ancient little wire-framed trailer hooked on, too.

Small dogs bit at his feet and small children snickered at him, but the boy didn't care. The more stops he made, the lighter his load grew and soon he was sailing along the narrow streets, the sun ahead of him, a warm wind on his face. He turned onto Shepherds Park, four deliveries to go and the Bottoms' house next.

It wasn't a nice place, half-brick, all dirty, everything in the garden dead or dying, a useless car on blocks in the drive. There was a rusted shed to one side, the front grown over with weedy vines. "Nice hat, squit." Nick Bottoms came to the door and grabbed the cap from Michael's head.

"Here's your Mom's groceries." Michael took the cap back.

"Awww, you got a job, poor swot," Nick laughed.

Michael said nothing.

"We're meeting tonight, seven, behind the mill."

"Sorry, Nick." The boy set the groceries down. "Can't hang with the boys anymore."

"Says who?"

"Magistrate," Michael told him.

"Why not?"

"He says I should do something worthwhile with my life," Michael answered.

"Who, you?!" Nick laughed again. Michael tried to back away, but Nick stayed with him. "Wearing a stupid hat and a vest is worthwhile?"

"I don't *have to* wear it," Michael said, though he did.

But Nick only laughed some more.

Michael went to the bike and said, "Okay. Seven tonight."

It was past six when he finished his deliveries and hung his vest and cap in the stockroom. He started for the lavatory when Myron said, "Uncle Fenn just finished in there. It'd kill an elephant, goin' in there."

"I need to pee," said Michael.

"Your funeral," Myron shrugged.

Michael headed to the Youth Court for his check-in. By the time he was done, at a quarter of seven, the staff had locked the courthouse toilets. He set out for the mill.

But somewhere between here and there, Michael set himself on another course. He had questions and wanted answers.

He went to the stone cottage.

A Blood Moon lit the crossroads, where everything was perfect and still. Michael needed to pee, a serious and overdue pee. He headed into the trees and heard the music— *that* music. He forgot his full bladder and followed the sound. As he moved out of the forest and toward the stone cottage, the melody floated in the air around him, over him, through him.

There wasn't a whisper of light from the little house. The old man was surely sleeping. Michael headed around to the rock-walled garden, choosing his steps carefully in the cold and unwelcoming dark. The stones were moss-slicked, but he found footholds and climbed the full ten feet. Along the top, torrents of red rose cascaded over and left the air thick and unreal. Michael tried to see into the garden, but a fat beech tree blocked his view.

The music was stronger now, pulling him. He climbed down the wall and the song stopped. He stepped around the wide beech and saw it.

Spread across the garden was a city, a whole other world in miniature: Thin cobbled streets snaked among stone houses whose roof peaks hardly reached the boy's chest. There was a slender-spired church, a tumbled row of almshouses, all glowing amber in the gaslight. There was a large town center, an open square where a small fountain burbled, and perfect little shopfronts with perfect-lettered signs. There were pubs, an inn, banks, offices.

The streets off the square led to more houses, some with minute and neatly tended gardens, others plain and bare. Wagons and carriages were parked here and there. A small gulley of a stream wandered past a manor house with a wide green, stables, outbuildings. He saw a broad pond glint in the distance.

The boy moved through a city that was complete in every impossible tiny detail. Who would have built such a thing? And why? Was it the old man? Was this how he spent his time, his money?

If Michael had money, he wouldn't waste it on this kind of nonsense. And that's what it was, nonsense. That's what he felt in his heart.

But in another second, and for the rest of his life, Michael wouldn't know what was and wasn't nonsense.

He was about to take the pee he needed when he heard a soft *clop-clopping* and a man no bigger than his fist came galloping on a horse the size of the boy's shoe. The horse reared and the little man yelled at the top of his little lungs: "Citizens, Friends, Brothers, Sisters—for the Honor of our Nantwuzzl'd Race—to arms!"

Shutters flapped open and People—little *People*, inches tall—appeared at every window, armed. They came at him from all directions, fired tiny guns, shot needly arrows, threw minuscule stones, they screamed, shouted, babbled at him. He would've laughed, but their bullets and arrows were real; they poked, pelted, pricked him like the sting of a thousand bees.

Even as they attacked, Michael saw the looks on their faces: wide, wondering looks, like children, afraid and curious at once. And he knew one thing. He knew that these little creatures, whatever-they-were, wanted him dead. If he stood there long enough, taking enough of their bullets and arrows, they'd kill him.

"Go away, you squits! Go away!" the boy called out.

They were charging him now, by the dozens, no, hundreds, and none more than a half-foot tall. Young and old, man, woman, child, they came at him from every corner—from every building, every house, darting down streets, jumping out of trees, everywhere, whole wagonloads of them, all of them armed, moving in for the kill.

Michael jumped back and tripped, tumbled down a small cobbled street. His head scraped the side of a church and his shoulder hit a streetlamp and knocked it over. A gas-fed fire spread to a hay wagon, then to a wattle-and-wood building.

The one on horseback turned and called: "Citizens, Friends, Brothers, Sisters! We must fight the whumpin-whompinous fire!" The first building burned fast and the flames took another structure. Michael watched the Little

Ones scrambling, alarms belling and fire wagons, all rickety and rocketing into the town center. But the conflagration was spreading and red rivers of flame flowed up still more walls.

One of them yelled at Michael, a bulb-bellied man in a cap, tiny arms flailing like a windmill. "Don't just stand there. Do SOMETHING, you great Blefuscudian Lump!"

The boy could think of only one thing and that was how much he needed to pee. He unzipped his trousers and let flow a warm gold stream. It flowed and flowed and the flames began to fall back, sizzling, fizzling, as he emptied his stretched bladder.

The little round man was caught in the back splash. "Great Ghost of Bolgolam!" he sputtered, he spat. "I'm DROWNING in his poison!"

Now the fire was in full retreat, doused and steaming, and the tiny People had a chance against it. The whole village came together in a bucket brigade and forgot Michael altogether.

He heard a dog's growl and saw the mountainous thing running at him, teeth flashing in the firelight, and the old man's voice from the cottage, "What's going on?" Michael ran for the wall. He climbed as fast as he could, the dog charging, snarling, snapping for his feet. "What's happening out there?"

The boy slipped on the damp stones, but kept his grip and kept climbing. His fingers were raw when he found the top and jumped. He landed hard in gravel on the other side, cutting his hands and his face. He ran into the night, with blood and pure panic stinging his eyes.

He ran back to the small flat and cleaned himself and locked himself in his room. And he sat there, asking himself: *What just happened to me? I had a dream, right? There weren't any little People, no little town. A weird dream. But I'm bleeding real blood. I didn't dream that part.*

Michael wanted to tell someone, but who? Not Freddie, never. Not his classmates, not Charlie, they'd think he was out of his mind. He went to find Nick and the Boys.

But when he got to the mill, they were gone. They had stopped waiting for him an hour ago and were breaking into cars now.

The next morning at school, Hetty Bellknap was talking about Captain Cook and his journey across unexplored seas. "Who remembers what year he set sail on his first voyage?"

Charlie leaned to whisper, "Your head's drippin' some blood."

Michael wiped it dry on his sleeve.

"It was 1768, Ms. Bellknap."

"That's right, Penelope Rees."

Penelope went on to share all she knew about James Cook and Michael's thoughts were on the things he'd seen the night before.

"What about Captain Cook's ship? Who can tell me the name?"

"*Enterprise*," sniffed Charlie.

"That was Captain Kirk's ship," said Penelope. "It was *Endeavour*. The word *endeavour* means 'to try.'"

"It does. And why do you imagine Captain Cook tried, what drove him to undertake that journey? He had a nice home, a fine family. It wasn't for money or fame. Why did he set out on such a dangerous voyage?"

For once, Penelope Rees had no answer.

"What do you think, Michael?" Hetty asked, but he didn't hear: his mind was still in the little city. "You want to know what I think? I think he did it because he had to," she went on. "I think something drove him to explore. There are those among us who are born with some light, some spark inside—a restless soul—a need to make the grand journeys, to have the beautiful adventures. Maybe James Cook didn't *belong* in a comfortable house. And maybe you, Michael," she set a hand on his shoulder, "belong in this classroom."

The rest of them laughed and his mind sailed back into the room. When school was done, Michael set out for the job at Fenn's. He stocked shelves and made deliveries and all he could think was this: What was that other world in the garden? And how could he get back to it?

CHAPTER SIX

◆

BRENDAN
THE VOYAGER

Michael put his schoolbooks on the stockroom shelf and started gathering groceries for delivery. Myron watched him, beady-eyed and resentful.

"I'll be leaving now, Myron," Michael said to him, "to make those deliveries."

"Knock yourself out," the other boy shrugged. "And I mean it. Knock—yourself—out."

This was the only part of the day Michael really liked, outside, on the bike, in the fresh air, free of Myron and his peppermint, free of everything. He was taking a shortcut, across the hillside, when he passed the old school, St. Brendan's.

It had been a shipbuilder's estate once, a mansion built in the Mogul style, with iron onion domes, fragile lattice, mysterious minarets and turrets. When this shipbuilder died with no heirs, the place became a hospital, then a hotel, then sat empty for a decade and finally ended up a school. There was a plaque near the front, put there by the Old Brendanites Society, with a bronze portrait of restless St. Brendan himself, the first great explorer, setting out in a boat of animal-skin to discover the world, with sails full of wind and dreams.

It wasn't an easy school: the days here were a full hour longer. And she was in there, he knew, that strawberry-haired girl from the car. A last bell rang and students poured out in their perfect uniforms—bloodred jackets, grey trousers, skirts—all healthy, all wealthy, like another race from another world. And then he saw her, the girl with the wondering eyes. She was walking with a friend.

"Not you again," she said when she saw him.

"Me again."

"Who is this?" the friend asked. "You know him?"

"Me and Dad have run into him before," the girl answered and to Michael she said, "I'm Jane."

"Hi," he said back. "My name's Michael."

Her friend looked at him and the old bike and said, "I'm thinking . . . you don't live around here."

"Nahhh," and he waved a hand. "Over that way, I guess."

Jane was about to say something more when her father called from the car: "We're in a hurry!"

"Have to go," she said, and, "Bye, Michael."

"Bye," he told her.

And when she was near the car, she stopped and called back, "See you around, I guess."

"I guess," he called to her.

Jane Teresa Mallery was not like Michael in a lot of ways and one was this: the course of her life had already been charted. She would graduate St. Brendan's near the head of her class, would go to the university, have a brief but successful career in business, choose a husband from a very short list; and when both of her children were at St. Brendan's, she would get involved with charitable organizations and do admirable work.

That was the life waiting for her, and she knew it, but she wasn't looking forward to it.

Mr. Fenn was hanging up the phone when Michael came in early the next morning, a Saturday. "Only one delivery today. For that— the crazy ol' loon."

In a quarter hour, Michael was ready and he set out. The bike was heavy, even the wire trailer full: there were dozens of tins, meat, dog food, a few bottles of scotch, and all sorts of cleaning supplies, soaps, brushes, and such.

Lemuel Gulliver, the order said. Fenn had told the boy to leave the groceries outside, on the step, don't knock, crazy loon likes his privacy, respect it.

When he got to the stone cottage, Michael knuckled the heavy oak door.

And he waited. And he waited. He pounded the door again.

At last, he heard movement inside.

When the door swung open Michael said, "I'm here with your groceries."

"You are."

"I can bring them in, if you like."

"All right then, bring them."

The boy stepped inside and was blind in a cool dim room. As he began to see, he saw that every inch held *something*, on every table, every shelf, in every corner, there was something. It was a museum, full of the treasures of one man's travel through life: scarabs from the Egyptian desert, tile mosaics from ancient Italy, carpet from a shah's palace, wood carvings of African bush spirits, a wide canvas of the American plains. There were stone devils from India, Chinese scroll-paintings, a blanket of wild goat hair and cedar bark, each a gift the old man had got on his journeys.

There were books all around, big, small, new books and old, kept-behind-glass books. There were maps pinned to walls, maps to places the boy didn't know were real or not. There was a globe as tall as he was, on a dark-wood base with legs like sea monsters. There were ships, in paintings, photographs. A complicated telescope stood by a fogged-over window. The room was full, not cluttered or chaotic, and Michael thought he could spend a year and not see it all.

The old man led the way and the boy took the first load of groceries to the kitchen. The floor was limestone flag, wide and uneven; the walls were whitewashed, or had been. An old iron range covered most of one side. Michael set the bags on a plank table, by a battered wartime cabinet.

He went back to the parlor, and the dog came at him from shadow. Michael jumped and fell against the globe and set it spinning.

"Come on, Whitby, settle," said Lemuel. "He's here to help, isn't he?" Mr. Gulliver rubbed the dog's huge head behind the eyes, and Whitby settled. "How much help, well, that remains to be seen." Michael went back, again and again, bicycle to kitchen, and the old man sat and drank.

Michael brought in the last of the delivery and stood there, dumbly. He wanted to say something, but couldn't think of anything.

The old man watched him. And drank.

Finally, the boy said, "My name's Michael. Michael Pine."

And the old man said, "I'm Lem. Lemuel Gulliver."

Michael turned when a new sound drifted in an open window. "You hear that? That music?"

Mr. Gulliver nodded.

"I heard it before," the boy said.

The old man only nodded.

"It's always the same. And it's never the same. It doesn't begin and it doesn't end."

Another nod.

"I wish I knew," Michael said and nearly to himself, "where it was coming from."

"All right, then." Lem Gulliver lifted himself from the chair, as if he'd decided something important. "You wish you knew and now you'll know. Come with me." The old man reached for a key on the back wall, a strange-looking key, ancient and rusted so black it almost glowed. "A very useful key, a key to *all* locks," he said as he opened the door and waves of sunlight washed the cottage.

They moved outside, down a brick path, and Michael followed the old man to the Garden City. It was bigger than he remembered, more houses, shops, churches than he'd seen the first time. The fire, too, was worse than he'd dreamed: across the town center, a dark scar of ruined buildings. What could be salvaged from these structures had been piled in sad sodden heaps by the stone fountain.

Beyond the fire-blackened buildings, the little village was untouched. Neat narrow streets ran to every unseen corner of the garden and there must have been a hundred houses. Much of it was built from the same stone as Michael's village, the same golden-wheat-colored stone. Roofs were rock tile, spotted with moss. The distant land was farm and there was a pond, wide as a lake by this scale, a small sailboat moored at a small dock.

The old man tapped his cane on a church bell. "Friends," he called out, "citizens, brothers, sisters," and his voice carried across the city and to the great stone wall that held it in. "You have a guest."

Windows and shutters and doors opened and People appeared: children, men, women, young, old, more than a hundred of them and the tallest half a foot high. A few had tiny dogs on little leashes. Michael was sure they knew him, from the night of the fire, but their small faces were hard to read.

"The music," said Lemuel, "is theirs."

The odd little things came in every shape, every size, short, tall, heavy, thin, well-groomed, rumpled. Their clothes seemed to be a cross between old Asian and European styles and all brightly colored. They kept a wary distance from the boy, except one: a little man late in middle-age, thick in the gut and a full reddish face. "Good afternoon, Quinbus Flestrin." It was the one Michael had seen on horseback that night.

"It's what they call me," Lem told the boy, "and what they've called all the Gullivers."

"Roughly meaning the 'Man Mountain,'" the little man went on, "in the *lingua franca,* that pidgin language binding our two great Races." He wore a naval uniform, full dress, royal red: a surtout, or frock coat, with white piping; lively tasseled epaulettes; a wide-set row of buttons down the front. He had a crisp white shirt, red breeches, white stockings, well-shined boots, and a sword swinging at the waist.

To top it off, he wore an amazing helmet, not from any uniform Michael knew, but wide-brimmed, made of pure gold, covered with jewels and tiny bird feathers decorating the crest.

"These are the People of Lesser Lilliput," said Lemuel, "and this is Burton Topgallant, the longest-serving of all their Grand Panjandrums."

Only the Grand Panjandrum could wear the Golden Helmet.

"Call me G.P., if you like, Prime Minister, President, Potentate, or Pooh-Bah," the little man went on, "Dispenser of Justice, Fighter for Truth, the Keeper of Hopes, Dasher of Dreams, the End-All, Be-All, and Admiral of the Fleet, I answer to any of these."

"What fleet?" Michael asked quietly.

"The admiralty is hereditary here," Lemuel answered. "A Panjandrum is elected whenever the mood strikes them."

The boy noticed another of them, a quiet young girl in a peasant smock, looking him over and making notes on the back of an envelope. "He's young," said Burra Dryth, and almost to herself. "I put him at fifteen *pidriffs* high, maybe weighing four dozen *rinniks*. That would make him no more than, say, 300, 350 *humjinks* old."

"But it's impossible," said another. "No giant can be that young."

"Doesn't make sense," from still another. "They're almost extinct, aren't they?"

"Or maybe," said the Grand Panjandrum, "the Ancient Texts have it wrong. Maybe more of them have survived than we dared imagine."

"I won't stand for this!" came a shrill and vigorous new voice. "Arrest the hooligan! Throw the Giant in *SHACKLES*!" Hoggish Butz looked like a very full tick. He had a fungus-like beard over all his chins, pinhole eyes and a nose like a bird's beak. He was the one Michael had left pee-soaked. "He's committed *HIGH TREASON*! The Blefuscudian Lump must be Hung, Drawn and Quartered! By the Great Ghost of Bolgolam, I demand it!" (The Lesser Lilliputians, especially when stressed, tended to lapse into this sort of Babble-Speak.)

"He's your friend," Lemuel said to them all. "He's come here to help you."

And at that, they moved closer, smiling shyly, waving warily, calling out greetings, sometimes in a language Michael knew, sometimes not. Some kept a safe distance and some reached to touch his trousers, unsure, cautious, while others climbed onto his shoes like eager, curious children.

And the boy could only wonder, what did the old man mean? How could *he*, Michael Pine, help anyone?

CHAPTER SEVEN

LIKE THE PHOENIX, REBORN

A h, crud," Freddie said when Nick came looking. "I don't know where the brat is an' I don't care."

"You tell him come see me."

"Tell him yourself." Freddie couldn't stand the sight of Nick Bottoms. Nick was another Freddie, but a lot younger and a lot better-looking. "He's not my kid. What's he mixed up in now?"

"Nothing you need to know. All I want to know is, where is he and why does he keep letting me down."

"I'll tell you this," Freddie said. "There's nothin' wrong with the brat that a good beatin' wouldn't fix. I'd do it myself, but they'd take him away and my three hundred pounds a month, too. You want to see him, tell him yourself. You want to keep him in line, beat him up a few times. Beat him up good, that's what he needs."

Nick Bottoms made a living selling what he stole, but business was down. Rumor was, Lyall Murphy and his Gang from Ambridge wanted to move into Moss-on-Stone. Lyall's Gang was doing well, marking their growing territory, tagging it 7-A-M, for Seven-Ambridge-Men.

Nick's Boys were barely hanging on.

"Let's rob that place with the old sisters," this from Gordy, who was nosing around in a rubbish bin behind the pub. "We never tried there before."

"It's a bookshop, y'twallop," said Peter.

"Well, how'm I s'posed to know," sniffed Gordy. "Nobody ever told me."

"We're going to hit one of the big places on the hill," Nick told them.

"Nah, Nick, not that," said Peter. The Boys had never broken into houses before. It was too risky. So many people had alarms and dogs these days. "Let's hit some cars."

"We can't keep doing the one thing," Nick said. "We have to try new things. That's how you get ahead, am I right?"

"Nick's right," from Phil, the only thing he said all night.

"Who goes in first?" Robby wanted to know.

"One thing's sure, it's not gonna be ol' Gordy," snorted ol' Gordy. "It was Gordy did all the car break-ins last night, wasn't it. Now it's somebody else's turn, am I right, Nick?"

"You're going in first," Nick told him. "Then Phil, and Peter."

"Ahhhh, c'mon, Nick! I get caught again, I'll go to YOI," said Gordy, one second before he nearly lost a fingertip to a trap meant for vermin.

"Then don't get caught," Nick said, and they climbed into his Dad's old Victor and went looking for houses to rob.

Burto▮ ▮▮ ▮allant, the Grand Panjandrum of Lesser Lilliput, clim▮▮▮ ▮ the tiny town fountain and called with all his voice▮ ▮▮ns, Brothers, Sisters—a friend of Flestrin is a friend ▮ ▮ryone! Welcome, Quinbus Ninneter!"

"Mea▮ ▮g, roughly, 'the Boy Mountain,'" Lem said.

"Great Ghost of Bolgolam," was all Hoggish Butz had to say as he left.

The G.P. declared this a New Quinbus Day and shops were closed and celebrating began. Tiny paper lanterns were strung from the branches of small trees, and tables were piled with mountains of food and drink: salmon in paper-thin slivers, roast lamb with mint sauce, little servings of fisherman pie and steak-and-kidney pudding, walnut short-bread, fresh peach in vanilla syrup, and magnums of the old wine they called *Glimigrim*. One of them tried to share her meal with Michael, but a full serving here filled half a human spoon and he took only enough to be polite.

Little men and little women started dancing when the orchestra played that music again. It was, Lemuel explained, their one eternal song: a serenade, a symphony, dance, dirge, always the same notes, never the same tune. As the music went on, with no beginning or end, the old man introduced the boy to more and still more of them.

There were Bankers, Bakers, Census-Takers, Schoolchildren, Teachers, Congregants, Preachers, Pipe-Fitters, House-Sitters, the wrong, the right, the profound and the trite. Evet Butz was a Farmer, a small man of few words and those not well-chosen. His brother Hoggish was round and L*OUD*, a self-obsessed Rouser of Rabble. Hoggish's one fr the Surgeon, Dr. Ethickless Knitbone, an edgy a rfed woman. He met gangly young Philament Phlopp, works Fanatic whose eyebrows had been singed so m y times, they'd stopped growing.

There were Students from a local public school; and Thudd Ickens, Bookkeeper and Amateur Acrobat; Upshard Tiddlin, Mother of Slack and Frigary; Mumraffian Rake, a Locksmith; the Editor of *The Scribblerus*; and more and still more. Lemuel took the boy past Mount Oontitump University, a fine campus, built on a mountain that had been a molehill. Michael met the Oontitumpity Dons in their billowing bell-shaped robes and bright green caps, distinguished-looking men, highly revered among themselves. These aged Dons had spent so many years together, they'd forgot the native tongue and spoke a dialect based on several dead languages.

The population averaged around two hundred over the years; there were a hundred ninety-three of them now. At least ten buildings had been lost to the fire Michael started; the Blood Moon Fire, they called it. Sixty shops and businesses remained, intact, untouched, in the town center. There were offices, a theatre, a museum, near a hundred houses in the neighborhoods beyond. Michael counted a half-dozen mills in the manufacturing district. A small resort sat on the shore of their lake.

The farthest land was farmed in tiny fields of wheat and barley, neatly marked by stone walls and hedgerows. Cattle the size of mice grazed here, and there were also horses, sheep, pigs, chickens, geese. Dogs and cats smaller than Michael's thumb were kept as pets, and he saw one caged bird no bigger than a housefly. The narrow tracks of a steam locomotive bound the Nation in an endless circle, and Eddish Rantipole sorted mail on the night train.

And the old stone wall held it all in.

You can ask almost any anthropologist and you will hear that *Culture is Cumulative*, that who we were makes us who we are. Through the centuries, these Lesser Lilliputians had evolved a society like and unlike our own: they were a fascinating and frustrating race, a jumble of endless contradictions. They were weak and they were strong, persevering and passive, resilient, fragile, resourceful, helpless, industrious, lazy, trivial and remarkable.

Their technology was primitive, at least a hundred years behind. They had no television, telephones, no computers; they were not wasteful; their air and waterways were clear.

Their outlook on life was quaint, old-fashioned: there was no crime, because they still felt shame; they admired common sense and didn't have lawyers. Cynicism, they knew, was the First Refuge of Scoundrels and they'd found that Incivility could be treated with Essence of Bergamot. They understood that Rights meant Responsibilities and Chocolate was better than War.

They were passionate about everything, full of big ideas. Whatever they did, they did with all their hearts, at least until their interest began to fade and they wandered on to new things. They were impulsive, impatient, curious and adventurous, the way children are.

Three centuries back, the original Lemuel Gulliver—the first Quinbus Flestrin—helped them craft a Constitution and its simple philosophies guided them still. The earliest copy had been damaged in the Blood Moon Fire, but Thudd Ickens saved it from burning entirely. Michael used a magnifying glass to read:

GREAT CHARTER OF LESSER LILLIPUT

March 20th in the yeare 1725

On this the Day of the Upended Egg, we establish a Sovereigne Nation of free People, on the territorye extending Twelve Hundred Glumgluffs by Fifty Blustrugs, and whose borders are described by Flestrin's Wall.

We, the Undersigned, confirme these Three Eternal Principles for Us & our Heirs, For Ever—

That We each finde a Course by a Common Compass.
That We only know that We do not know.
And that no Journey has an End.

And that was it, half a page long. All their laws and philosophies, all their hopes and dreams were held in those words. There was no reason to put anything more to paper.

Flestrin's Wall, as Michael learned, was built by the first Lemuel Gulliver to protect the Little Ones from the world beyond. Over time, the People came to fear everything past it and legends grew as legends do.

They dreamed of a cruel and merciless place outside the Wall—and they called it the Land of Naught and Nil, a nightmare world, bleak and barren, where life could not thrive. According to their Ancient Texts, this world was inhabited by a few last Giants, straggling survivors of a lost, doomed race, tormented by bloodthirsty monsters. The first Gulliver let their own fear keep them here, safe, inside the Wall.

"But how," Michael asked the old man, "how can I help them?"

It was the Grand Panjandrum who answered: "You will assist Quinbus Flestrin. You will help watch over our Sovereign Nation and help restore what we have lost."

And that's what happened. Michael came to the Garden City each day and made right the wrong he'd done. He cleared the scorched remains of old buildings and swept the foundations clear.

The Lesser Lilliputians decided to build a Great Hall, stone and fireproof, in the empty space left by the fire. It would be a library, theatre, seat of government, a gathering place for them all, and home to the Sacred Vault. This vault, as Michael learned, held a never-seen relic called the Inevitable MaGuffin of Lesser Lilliput.

"This," Topgallant explained, "is the *First & Only Secret*, the Solution to the Infinite Enigma, the Unraveling of the Eternal Conundrum, the Resolution to the Ever-Lasting Riddle, the One Answer to All Questions: why are we here, where have we come from, where are we destined to go, and so on and so forth."

"But what exactly," Michael asked, "is this thing?"

"We don't *exactly* know," one answered. "It's a mystery and that's the point."

"Oh, we tried to get in there, to take a look, but we couldn't," from another.

"It's locked, you see," added Philament Phlopp, the one with no eyebrows. "Not even Mumraffian Rake, greatest locksmith in all Lesser Lilliput, can open it."

"But if you never saw what's in there," Michael went on, "how do you know for a fact what it is?"

The Grand Panjandrum stepped in to explain: "You ask the wrong question, Brother Ninneter. We know nothing for a *fact*. Facts are fungible, troublesome things. We don't put much faith in them."

"And neither should you," said another.

"We know it holds the Answer, because we *know* it holds the answer," this from one named Fammel Plushes.

"And just because we haven't gotten the vault open," the Grand Panjandrum went on, "doesn't mean the Answer isn't there, isn't real. A shoe, cat, sunset, heartache—these things are real, we know that. It takes no particular effort to accept them as such. But the unseen and un-seeable and never-known things, those take a bit of working at. And those are the things most worth believing."

It was late-autumn now and the days were dropping away as fast as the beech leaves, the nights stretching cold and windy. The boy kept at his job and was mostly happy: he liked the work and liked harmless Mr. Fenn. But Myron was something else. Myron hated Michael and did everything he could to make the boy quit the market.

Michael just ignored him and that made Myron madder still.

And when, on a wet Tuesday in early November, Myron found that his uncle was going to raise Michael's salary, he grew dizzy with rage.

"*I* ask you for a raise and you say you can't afford it!" Myron screamed at his uncle.

"That's right," replied Fenn.

Myron thought he would pass out or throw up or both. "Then how can you afford it for *him*?!"

"Easy," Fenn answered. "I'm takin' it out of your pay."

This couldn't go on, Myron knew that. He unwrapped another peppermint stick and decided to get rid of that boy, one way or another.

The People of the Garden City held a competition, open to everyone, to find a design for the Great Hall. Soon, blueprints and models began to arrive and these were shown in a tent in the town center. There were submissions from Artists, Accountants, Daydreamers, Professors of Engineering, and these were impressive things, like castles, cathedrals, mammoth structures of stone, with heavy buttressed walls.

The Lesser Lilliputians came each day to marvel at each new design and none of them looked more closely than the little peasant girl, Burra Dryth. She had been born to the poorest family in the village; for her first ten years, she hardly spoke, but only watched. And as she watched, she missed *nothing*.

Everyone waited for the last model, from the Dean of the Architects. When it arrived, the whole village came to see. His design was remarkable, spectacular, *nantwuzzl'd* to use their word, a building for the ages!

Burra studied the model and listened to the People praise it. But she wasn't as sure; she wondered if it wasn't a monument to the Architect himself, not a place for them all. A new dream began to take hold in her young head and she hurried home to sketch it on paper. Burra knew nothing of designing buildings, but set to teaching herself. She read every book, studied every structure in the city.

And then she went to work. She started making that dream in her head.

Word got around what Burra was doing and the People of Lesser Lilliput shared a few laughs. Burra Dryth, imagine! The odd little rag-girl! What was she thinking?!

The Artists and Professors weren't amused: the thought of their models next to one from that peasant girl . . . it was *unthinkable!* They threatened to withdraw, but the Grand

Panjandrum calmed them. Only days remained and the competition would be closed, he reminded them. Young Miss Dryth would surely tire of the project before then.

But Burra spent every minute working, all day and all through the night. She couldn't afford proper materials and built her model from scraps she scavenged in the village, from cardboard and kindling. When she was at last done, she brought it to the town center. A crowd gathered for another good laugh.

But there was no laughter that day.

Her model was unlike anything they'd ever seen: simple, graceful, beautiful, it towered over the others in every way. Its slender walls were cut with long flowing windows, as lively as waterfalls, rising from the ground to an immense stone-tiled dome. The thing was colossal and delicate, majestic, yet welcoming, vast and personal, classical and revolutionary; like their music, it was many ideas at once.

"But this is ridiculous!" someone snorted. "Un*build*able!" another sniffed. Those walls will never support the dome! The whole thing will crash down and kill everyone inside!

But the Dean of the Architects studied Burra's work and checked each dimension, calculating, recalculating, testing its engineering and the stresses it could hold. The structure, he finally announced, was sound. Burra Dryth had designed a perfect building. In a show of respect, he removed his own model from the competition and Burra was chosen the winner.

Work began right away. A building this size would need all their effort. They would hew massive timbers, carve giant columns, cast thousands of tiles. Michael helped as he could, chiseling stones into blocks. He worked every day until his hands were cramped and blistered.

One day, a Tuesday, he lost all track of time. He stayed too long, making stacks of blocks, and was about to be late for his Court check-in. He raced from the garden and ran the miles back to Moss-on-Stone.

He was running up Sheep Street when Nick and the Boys found him and boxed him in the narrow lane. "We need to talk."

"Can't talk now, Nick. I'm going to be late." The town bell was ringing six fifteen.

But Nick needed to know: "Why do you keep letting me down?"

CHAPTER EIGHT

THE MAHARAJA'S DAUGHTER

A police car slowed and swept its spotlight over the dim street. The Boys slipped into shadow and Nick called from the dark, "Last chance, you dumb squit. Be at the mill tonight, ten o'clock."

Michael hurried on to the Court and was there in time for check-in, barely. He was home and in bed and asleep by nine. When he didn't show at the mill at ten, ten thirty, or eleven, Nick angrily told the Boys they'd deal with him later.

They were hitting another big house on the hill; Peter had checked it and found the owners were away on holiday. The place was long and narrow and golden stone, set close to the street, a long hedge to one side. Nick waited down the block in the old Victor, and the Boys set to work on a window. They jimmied it partway, but it wouldn't go wider. Michael could've slipped through with no problem, but it was a tight fit for the rest of them.

Phil and Peter got in, but Gordy's thick gut wedged him tight. "Somebody help me," he squealed.

"What's your problem?" Peter snapped.

"I'm stuck, for God's sake! Can't you see I'm *stuuuck*!" Gordy squealed.

"Stop squealing," Phil told him.

"I'm not squealing!" Gordy squealed again.

The house was empty, Peter was right about that. Except for the German Shepherd. The dog hadn't taken a holiday. Gordy's squeals brought it running. It raced for the Boys and they ran for the nearest door. But Gordy was still jammed in the window and the dog turned on him. Now the barking and screaming brought the whole neighborhood. Nick didn't wait, but took off in the old car.

Police flooded the street in short minutes. Peter and Phil got away, but Gordy only got a face full of dog bites and a year in YOI.

Nick drove all the way to the crossroads. He turned off the engine and sat in the car and pounded the dash. Why was this happening? He was losing control of everything; nothing was going right for him. Michael wouldn't have gotten stuck in that window. It would've been all right if *he'd* been here to help. Nick had put a lot of time and effort into the kid, and Michael kept letting him down.

Maybe Freddie was right: maybe the boy needed a good beating.

When Michael went back to the cottage the next day, he found Lemuel in a far corner of the back garden, where the little farms gave way to forest, clearing late-autumn leaves from the wall drains. It was a chore he had to keep up.

"If this gets blocked in a hard rain," he said, "the whole city will be underwater."

The two of them carried leaves and twigs from the garden. Michael went looking for a wheelbarrow, but found none. He tried the barn, but its doors were padlocked. He asked Lemuel if there might be one in the barn and the old man said no, there was only a car in there.

"A car? I didn't know you drove."

"Never have, never will."

"Then why," the boy asked, "do you have one?"

Lemuel answered with this story.

"When I was young, I captained my own ship, one of the last on the India route. It was mid-July as I set off on another voyage. The sailing was smooth at first and my ship soon rounded the African Cape. We were in the middle of a calm sea when the monsoon hit and the whole ocean turned on us. The storm thundered across the water like a thousand horses. Clouds as big as mountains hid the sun, the air turned bitter cold, and the rain hit like hornet stings. Gale winds lifted the waves higher and higher still, each peak shredding into foam. Lightning came in blinding blasts and rattled every plank of the ship, every bone in my body.

"I called the crew to haul up the foresail and square the yards as we raced over one wind-driven swell and into the deep trough below. We were blown miles off-course, but there was nothing we could do. We went where the storm took us. My men climbed the rain-slicked rat lines and clung to the yardarms and pulled in more sail; but even then, it was too late. The wind was driving us onto a rocky shore.

"By dawn, the worst of the monsoon had passed. We'd been blown halfway up a beach, the mainmast splintered and barely standing. But we were alive, not a man lost.

"Some farmers took me and my crew by ox-cart to the nearest village, and I hired woodworkers to repair the ship. As my crew settled in for a long wait, I decided to explore. I set off one morning, alone, into the wilderness, through a steaming rhododendron jungle, under tamarind trees full of screaming parrots and monkeys, and across hot mud-thickened rivers flowing with crocodiles.

"As I moved through a narrow canyon, I began to hear a sound, a strange new sound, a music like I'd never heard. I followed and it led me through an overgrown pass, where the mountain walls opened onto a plain. There was some-thing here, mostly lost to trees and jungle vine. If I hadn't looked twice, I might not've seen it.

"It was a temple, hid in the wild growth, a hundred feet high and half a mile wide, carved from one mountainous rock, thousands of years ago. It was so old, its gods had been forgotten. The entrance was flanked by sixty-foot stone Elephant Kings, settled on haunches, trunks raised in trumpet, crowns on their great smiling heads. The rest of the façade was a maze of dancing monkeys, some real, some not. And still there was the music, coming from within the temple.

"I had a lantern with me and made my way into an over-powering dark where night snakes hunted as they liked. I chased away a krait, small, deadly thing, and went deeper into the man-carved cave, following where the music led. The air was cooler here by twenty degrees and a few mon-keys followed me in, but lost interest soon enough. I moved down a long corridor, lined with angry stone tigers.

"Next, I came to a domed chamber, full of bat-smell and lit by candles. Dancers spun across every surface, as they had since the day they were carved. It was an other-worldly place, quiet and still. There is a word here, *nirvana,* for heaven, perfection, and it can be translated as 'beyond the wind.' And that's what this was: a perfect place, beyond all wind.

"In the middle of the room, surrounded by a hundred flickering candles, a young woman sat playing a flute. It was an extraordinary music, with no beginning or end. I stood there listening for a long time before she turned and saw me.

"She started to scream, but smiled. I learned that her name was Maya and she came to this place to practice the music she composed. The perfect dome played her song back in echo and she studied its sound. Her father, a Maharajah, had brought her here earlier that day. He was off on a tiger hunt, and she chose to stay and make music in the old temple.

"Maya was as beautiful as the melody she played, still and serene, dark-haired, with emerald eyes that seemed set on some distant future. She didn't wear the red bindi on her forehead, mark of a married woman.

"I was about to speak when we were both knocked from our feet. Our candlelight went out and we were blind in that windless dark. It was an earthquake, the worst in three hundred years, and the cave began to crumble around us. I found my way to Maya and realized she was hurt, her leg near crushed under falling stone. I carried her, climbing over rubble, both of us fighting to breathe the dirt-thick air. Each step seemed to take an hour, and the next one longer. But, in time, we saw a dim gold glow—last rays of a setting sun—and I went toward it.

"We were hardly out when the shrine collapsed, great Elephant Kings peeling away and crashing to bright dust. Her white dress was orange, dyed by dirt and sweat and blood.

"The night came fast and Maya was falling in and out of consciousness. I knew she needed a doctor, and soon. Landslides had blocked our path from the canyon, and I had to carry her up an unsteady rock slope.

"We were out of the canyon and surrounded by jungle—dark and alive with animal sounds, every creature in mindless panic. Tigers were passing a few feet away, running from a fear they'd never known. Maya was unconscious again and I had no idea where we were or should go. I was lost, without map or compass.

"Her father found us then. When the earthquake hit, he and his entourage of forty, all on elephant, came charging back. A Mahout, an elephant driver, helped settle Maya in the covered howdah and we began the journey home.

"The Maharaja's palace, untouched by the quake, was built of brilliant marble and set on an island in a man-made lake. A gold-and-ivory-trimmed barge carried us to it. The infirmary here was better than many hospitals, and a team of personal doctors set Maya's leg.

"The Maharaja was grateful to me for saving his one child, and he offered me many gifts. I thanked him, but turned these down. Not long after, my ship was repaired and I sailed home and forgot about the Maharaja—but I never forgot his daughter.

"Then, on a stormy afternoon the following spring, a truck showed up at the farm with a crate, from Bois-Colombes, in France. The Maharaja had ordered a motor-car built for me. Three hundred horsepower, fourteen feet long, an incredible Hispano-Suiza, full of carved ivory and rosewood. The company called it *Adventure*, after my ship. There were plans to build more, but it was too expensive to make in mass. So I had—I have—the only one. Never drove it, never learned how. But it's still there, in the barn, in the crate."

"Did you go back?" the boy wanted to know. "Did you see her again?"

CHAPTER NINE

◆

THE 27th ARTICLE OF WAR

That's another story," Lem answered, "for another time."

Over the days and weeks that came, the boy stayed busy helping the Little Ones rebuild their city. Burra Dryth's design for the Great Hall was rising in the town center. When Michael had cut enough stone, he left the Construction Crews to their work. He wandered the little town and found jobs that needed doing: he shoveled the gulley that ran through the Nation, raked the Farmer's fields of cut hay, and re-roofed the church spire.

The more he learned about these People, the more curious he became and the more he wanted to understand them.

He saw how most of them met life without complaint: when things went wrong, they didn't look for anyone to blame. They didn't curse or celebrate their fate, but took the good and the bad and went on.

When he was around them, the problems in his own life didn't seem as big. If they could get by, even thrive, so could he.

For their part, the Lesser Lilliputians were fascinated and confused by the new giant. They wrote books about him, taught classes on him at the University, even had a musical play based on him. They knew what they needed from Michael, but they wondered if he could really give it.

Some days, when the weather was cold or the Little Ones were taking a holiday, Michael helped Lemuel clean the old cottage. "I've lost control of this house," he said. "I need to get it in order."

Together, they cleared over-packed shelves and sorted papers. The old man asked about Mr. Fenn and the boy said he was fine, a fine little ordinary man. "But not too ordinary," said Lemuel. "He started the Parish Pantry and that wasn't ordinary at all."

Michael had been to the Pantry many times. Each week, grocers in the county gathered unsold goods, food near the end of its shelf time, and took it to the church where it was given to anyone who needed it. "That was Mr. Fenn's doing. He made the whole thing happen." Michael had never known this. "Sometimes, you have to look twice to see real worth," Lem was saying when an awful sound rose in the garden: a donkey's panicked braying, wretched as a rusted gate.

The old man called for Michael to get the gun.

When the little Farmer shouldered open the door of his barn, he found huge hideous monsters eating his geese and prized pig. He'd never seen anything like these grisly beasts, each bigger than two of his horses together. They darted at him, screeching and snapping their sharp wet teeth. Evet Butz grabbed a rifle and fired and reloaded and fired again, and again and again, but hit only hay. With angry hisses and barks, the creatures slid into dark corners of the barn. But he could see their breath in the cold, still air.

Philament Phlopp was near and heard the gunshots and livestock squeals. He came running and found a scythe and helped Evet fight off the beasts.

"What are these things?!" the Farmer cried. "Where'd they come from?!"

As they flushed the creatures from the barn, Phlopp called back, "I guess they're from over the Wall. I always thought they were a myth. But just look at them . . . !"

In fact, they were common weasels. *Mustela nivalis*, by the Latin name, among the smallest carnivores, cousin of the stoat, and often found around farms. Usually night hunters, weasels were sometimes active in the daylight, too.

It had been years, decades, whole Lilliputional generations, since one had dared to cross Flestrin's Wall.

Before this, the worst the People had to fear were the Sparrow Hawks. Two centuries before, the Little Ones built a stone tower and assigned a lookout to warn when a hawk-shadow crossed the sky. When the tower bell rang, they knew to run for the shelters. They were careful and cautious, and no one had been lost in a hundred and fifty years.

But the weasels were new, and the weasels were different.

Phlopp went running and yelling for the Tower Watch to sound the alarm, man, sound the alarm! As the bells began pealing, the People dropped what they were doing and hurried to the underground rooms they'd built around the city. There were hundreds, maybe a thousand shelters, expertly hidden: false rubbish bins held ladders to subterranean dens, plaster tree stumps hid chutes, some public toilets were portals to a hideaway. Every Little One heard the alarm and took refuge. Schoolchildren knew the drill and marched, single file, to the basement. Meals sat half-eaten on tables and life simply stopped. Lesser Lilliput was abandoned in seconds.

Lemuel and Michael found the weasels racing madly around the town square. The old man fired once, twice, three times and left three weasels dead and bleeding by the fountain. The dog Whitby carried them from the garden, one after the other, and the little town slowly came back.

News of what happened to the farm animals moved quickly through the city. For the first time in their history, Flestrin's Wall had failed them. For the first time in memory, monsters straight from the Land of Naught and Nil had invaded the Sovereign Nation of Lesser Lilliput.

Burton Topgallant couldn't speak the thoughts echoing around his head: when the weasels were done eating the Farmer's livestock, they'd move on to the villagers themselves.

"These People have always been safe here," Lemuel told the boy. "They are small and vulnerable and take care of themselves as best they can. Still, they can only do so much."

The old man settled into a chair and Michael saw it had taken a lot out of him. He was pale and his breath was loud and raw: "It's getting late. You'd better be going."

"You're not going to stay here all night."

"No sleeping on watch," said Lem. "Twenty-seventh Article of War forbids it."

"Isn't there some other way?" the boy asked. "It'll be cold and wet and . . ."

But Lemuel didn't answer and Michael left.

Snow fell that weekend, mounding by tree trunks and walls, dangerous drifts at a Lilliputian scale. Michael came on Sunday to sweep the garden clear, moving street to street. Pale ribbons of smoke rose from chimneys across the city. The Great Hall stood half-built, open to the weather, its dome unfinished. These days were too cold for the Little Ones. What was a chill to Michael could mean much worse for a race this small.

He was sure there was something *more* he could do, some better way to help them. But he didn't know what it was.

The Lesser Lilliputians kept mostly to their houses, day after arctic day. Cooped and cramped, their tempers grew sharp and short. They argued over meaningless things and forgot all that mattered.

Hoggish Butz spent the long nights alone, counting up the slights that had been done to him. Take the Great Hall— what a monumental waste of time and energy! Nobody asked his opinion. It was Topgallant who was behind that. How had *he* become Grand Panjandrum, and not Hoggish?

One such night, Dr. Ethickless Knitbone brought a nice Dunch Dump Pudding and Hoggish shared his bitter thoughts with her. "It makes no sense!" he howled as he ate. "Why should *THAT FOOL* wear the Golden Helmet!?" he yowled as he ate. "It's not fair!" He dropped his head to the table in a puddle of sour tears.

But the sobbing slowed as Dr. Knitbone said, "Burton Topgallant is a bogglesome nobkin."

"Bogglesome nobkin?! He's a Blefuscudian Lump!" (*Blefuscudian*, a term of uncertain origin, was probably meant as an insult to one's lineage.)

"Precisely," she told him, "and we both know it."

"Yes, Dr. Knitbone, dear. I know it and you know it, but THEY don't know it! Oh, the unholy THEM, the great unwashed rabble, the mindless masses, the ill-bred and easily led!"

Hoggish had given himself a Nervous Stomach now and he took to his great sagging bed, calling for Knitbone to bring the pudding and quickly, dear, quickly.

"The other day, I had a long talk with Topgallant," she said to him, soothing him. "I could tell he was uncomfortable being around someone of my intellect. So I took his hand in mine, holding it gently, you see, stroking it softly, as one would a stupid cat," she said, she soothed. "I looked in his eye and what did I see, Hoggish?"

"What did you see, dear Dr. Knitbone?"

"I saw a man with the I.Q. of a worm!"

"A WORM!" Hoggish gasped. "And not a smart one, I imagine."

The doctor nodded. "Not smart at all."

"Why don't the others see these things!?" cried Hoggish and his great gut bubbled and burbled.

"We see the truth. The others see what they are told to see."

"They are dumb!" Hoggish wept. "Dumb, dumb, dumb!"

"As always," Knitbone nodded, "your insights are keen and to-the-point."

"Drown the World! I should be Grand Panjandrum. I should wear the Golden Helmet!" He swallowed a wad of pudding.

Knitbone nodded again and said, "The Golden Helmet was *made* for your head," and she stroked that head as one would a stupid cat. "You are no one's fool, Hoggish Butz."

"No one's!"

"You are cunning, clever. You are independent, a free-thinker. Intellectual, cerebral!"

"I'm cunning, clever, a freethinker!" he shouted. "I'm— I'm— those other things you said."

She fed him still more pudding and said, "I've been thinking, Hoggish, and I have come up with a plan. If you do as I tell you, the Golden Helmet will soon be yours."

"I will, Dr. Knitbone, I'll do just as you say!" said Hoggish, eyes wide and wet with joy. "Tell me, please! What is our plan . . . ?"

CHAPTER TEN

———— ✦ ————

THE GREAT DUNCH DUMP CONSPIRACY

Hoggish Butz leaned close to hear every wonderful word as she laid out her scheme in that quiet room on that cold night. In time, the Lilliputian histories would remember it as the Dunch Dump Conspiracy. For now, it was only Dr. Ethickless Knitbone's nasty plot to remove the Golden Helmet from Burton Topgallant's head.

The scheme was simple, the scheme was this: Hoggish would begin chipping away at the others' confidence in Topgallant, cautiously, carefully, *cunningly*—a biting comment here, some cutting criticism there, a few droll rolls of the eyes. He would undermine everyone's faith in the man, stealthily and steadily, and he'd be so subtle about it, no one would know what he was doing.

Then, with the coming of Spring, Hoggish would make his move. He would call for a new election—*anyone* could do that—and with some creative vote-counting, if needed, he would claim his rightful role as the Grand Panjandrum of Lesser Lilliput.

The next morning, Christmas Eve, the Market was busy, noisy and alive with late shoppers buying up sauces and spices and all the overlooked things that make a holiday dinner. Fenn and Michael, even Myron, worked hard to keep up with the crowd. When the noon bell rang at St. Edwards, Fenn closed the doors and called Michael to the storeroom.

Myron followed and Fenn turned on the lights and there was the red 21-speed from Gadbury's. "Yours," he told Michael.

"*Whatdoyoumeanhis?!*" wailed Myron. "What about—me?!"

"What do you need with a bike? He's only, what, ten?" Fenn coughed and told them both to go home and have a good Christmas.

And Michael said, "Thank you." And, "I'm twelve."

He took the new bike on a long wandering course through the village. He flew through the Market Square, past Gadbury's, past the Bookshop. He rode by the Youth Court and up the hill, where the big houses were. He saw the girl named Jane getting in her father's car. He waved to her and nearly drove the bike into a tree.

When she waved back, her father asked, "Who's that?"

"His name's Michael," she told him.

"Who ran under the car," Mr. Mallery remembered.

"Yes, that's him."

"I've known kids like him," her father went on. "They never go anywhere, never change, never grow. One day, he'll wake up and be forty and right where he is now."

After he'd checked in with the Court, Michael rode to Lemuel's cottage. The streets of Lesser Lilliput, empty under the light snow, had been decorated for the holiday. Everything was strung with garland and light, tiny wreaths on tiny doors, and a three foot tree in the town center, heavy with ornament.

He found some of them in the parlor of a house, bundling into costumes, Upshard Tiddlin adjusting each one, adding touches to their made-up faces. From the Topgallant house, not far away, came the sounds of a lively party: cider scent and music, *that* music, filled the cold air.

Michael knelt in the snowy street and watched a dozen Little Ones, all in costume, slip through back alleys and gardens, laughing like schoolchildren. They ran the short blocks to the Topgallants' and pounded the door.

"Come, come," they called, "let the mummers in!"

The door was opened to them and they were greeted with food and drink and they began a noisy little play. One of them, dressed as Santa Claus, cried out: "Here I am, good Father Christmas, am I welcome or not? Don't tell me that Christmas has been forgot!" All the children of Lesser Lilliput swarmed as he tossed hard candy among them.

There was music, magic, juggling. Frigary Tiddlin tried reciting a holiday poem, but had a fit of giggling and left the room, red-faced. Everyone clapped anyway and Hoggish raised a glass and said:

"A toast to our Host! To the Grand Panjandrum! Mm, fine cider, Ms. Topgallant. And you made it nice and watery so it wouldn't run out like last year. Join me, friends. In this time of Peace, Love, and Joy, let's toast the man who has kept us safe! Well— never mind the awful fire that nearly KILLED us all. And, of course, the little incident with those monstrous CREATURES from beyond the Wall. We can't expect too much of him, can we? He is only a man, no better or worse than any of you."

There were some coughs, some shuffling and foot-scuffing in the uneasy silence that followed. Then, someone thankfully clattered a bell and called them to dinner and brought the whole awkward thing to an end. But Hoggish didn't care. It was a first step. He was sowing the seeds of doubt. And in time, those seeds would bear fruit.

A new fire was stoked and the Lesser Lilliputians feasted on tiny servings of boiled beef and veal, buns, grilled Barnsley lamb, cheeses, dumplings, cake; and they sang a Christmas carol set to their one eternal tune.

As Michael was leaving that night, he turned to look at the fat moon rising by the chimney, by the old empty nest. "It's a stork nest," Lemuel told him. "Maybe the only pair left in the country. They spend their winters in Africa, a thousand miles from here, but they always come home." And, he added, "A stork on the roof is good luck, you know."

"You never told me the rest of the story," Michael said, "about what happened to the girl in the palace."

"No," said Lemuel, "I didn't." And now he did.

"I sent many letters to the Maharaja's floating island, but none were answered. There was no way to know if she'd got them. After half a year, I decided to go back and talk to her myself.

"The Maharaja welcomed me and gave me a suite of rooms overlooking the lake. The next morning, I asked Maya to come back with me, to marry me.

"It was then she told me she would be married at the end of that month, to a man she'd never met. It was a different time and place, and these marriages were arranged almost at birth. Maya had no say in it. She begged her father, but it had all been settled, long ago. She'd meet her husband on the wedding day.

"I asked the Maharaja to stop the marriage and asked for his daughter's hand. He told me that I should leave and not come back or I'd be killed on sight. Three of his guards took me to the port city that night.

"But I did go back. At the edge of the compound, there lived a very old man—a Mahar, blinded and crippled in a battle long ago. He was the gatekeeper and kept track of all who came and went. He knew the Maharaja's order and knew he'd be the one to kill me. He asked why I'd come, knowing I'd die. I told him the simple truth, that I had no choice but to return.

"The old Mahar took pity on me and sent a message by Maya's maid, his wife. She's the one who helped spirit me past the guards and into the palace.

"On a small balcony above the lake, I once again asked Maya to come with me. She wanted to go, but was scared. She was sure that her father, the great tiger hunter, would track us down no matter where we went and have us both killed.

"And so, finally, I left and brought nothing with me but her music."

"Her music?" Only then did Michael realize that the little band was still playing in the back garden.

"That I'd heard in the stone temple, the music you hear now. I remembered it and taught it to the People here. As long as they keep playing, her song won't end."

It was after six when the boy reached the crossroads, where he waited for a car to pass. But the car didn't pass. Its head-lamps shone hard in his eyes and he heard doors open behind the glare.

"Been lookin' for you." It was Robby. Nick and the other Boys stepped up as Michael got off the bike.

"Hey, Nick," Michael said quietly. "Hey, guys."

"We're not all here, are we?" said Phil.

"Gordy's gone, squire," said Peter.

"'Cause of you," Robby put in.

"Me? What'd I do?" said Michael. "I didn't do anything."

"That's right," from Nick. "You didn't do anything but let us down again. If you'd been there like you promised, he wouldn't have got caught."

"No, I told you, Nick," Michael started, "I can't hang with—"

"Got a present for you," said Nick and he gave the Boys a nod and they gave Michael a bloody beating. They went at him with feet and fists, all four of them. Robby caught him square in the face and blood blasted from his nose and he felt an eye swelling shut. Phil hit him in the ribs, again and again, and he could hardly breathe. Someone got him in the back of the head and he fell into muddy snow.

"That's enough, eh, Nick?" one of them said.

"Is he still conscious?" said Nick.

"Yeah."

"Then it's not enough." Nick kept punching and kicking and might not have stopped, except another car was coming.

Michael wasn't conscious by the time the dark car drove up, and Nick and the Boys scattered in the night.

"Is he all right?" the girl asked.

"Get back in the car, Jane. I'll call for an ambulance."

But she brought a blanket for Michael and waited with her father.

When the hospital doctor had him cleaned and stitched, Stanley Ford stepped into the pale room. "Want to tell me what happened, son?"

"Wrecked," the boy answered. "My bike."

And the nurse said, "Mm-hm."

"Want to tell me what really happened?"

But he didn't tell. He lay two days in the hospital bed, both eyes blackened, ribs bruised but not broken. The Little Ones needed him and he wasn't there for them. He'd finally found something to care about, beyond his own small needs, and here he was stuck in a smelly bed in a smelly room with butter-colored walls.

Maxine Bellknap stood outside Folk-in-the-Clover, watching her breath hang in the cold air. Inside, Bertram, the wiry cook, brought the Chief Magistrate's dinner of pig's nose with parsley-and-onion sauce.

As the town bell struck seven, Horace Ackerby II began to eat by the chattering fire, looking out on the churchyard, listening to the wind in the yews. Maxine found her nerve and went to his table and said, "Mr. Ackerby. I'm sorry to bother you. And of course, I never would. But."

The Magistrate set down his fork. "What is it, Ms. Bellknap?"

"Well. Then. The boy. Michael Pine." The Magistrate was listening now. "Officer Ford says he was taken. The boy was taken. To the hospital, in a bad way, a slight concussion. He told Stanley it was a bicycle accident. But of course."

"Of course it wasn't."

Maxine wished she'd never come, wished she were home in a warm robe, with a pot of tea and gardening magazines, choosing spring seeds to order.

"He wouldn't say what happened. Still I thought. You should know."

For a very long moment, Ackerby said nothing.

"Thank you, Ms. Bellknap."

"Well, then," Maxine said and they said their good-byes.

The Chief Magistrate chewed at his food, slowly, and fell into a silent solitary rage. A street fight, a gang brawl. And after he, Horace Ackerby II, had taken such a chance on the boy. After all the time and effort he'd invested.

Should he end the experiment now? Should he swallow his sizable pride and send Michael to the YOI where he belonged?

CHAPTER ELEVEN

THE DAY OF
THE UPENDED EGG

Charlie Ford, the policeman's son, told Jimmy Bennet, and Penelope Rees overheard and told her mother, who called Frances Froth and that's how Mr. Tiswas found out and let Gadbury know and once Esther and Stella got the news, *everybody* knew what happened at the crossroads. Gang warfare, in their own city, and one boy in the hospital with a concussion!

The people of Moss-on-Stone knew they had a problem and they knew it was Nick and his Boys. "The most pernicious race of odious little vermin that nature ever suffered to crawl upon the surface of the earth," Stella called them.

Stella and Esther decided to start a Merchants Watch Committee. The business owners would keep an eye on each other's shops, taking turns patrolling the streets. It was a shame it had to happen in a village like theirs, but what choice was left?

On Wednesday, Michael was well enough for school, but still bandaged and bruised and sore. His teacher, once more, did not call attention to him but went on with their studies of the explorer Captain Cook:

"As his ship *Endeavour* rounded the tip of South America, it reached that point where two great currents converge, where Atlantic and Pacific Oceans meet. The seas are unpredictable here and violent storms explode with no warning. Cook's sails were filling with a deadly wind . . ."

Charlie leaned to Michael and sniffled, "I have a fifty pound note in my shoe. My nan gave it to me for not failing school. You want t'see it?"

Michael shook his head, no. Charlie was always coming up with stories like that.

"You want, I'll show you," Charlie whispered. "Anytime."

And Michael said, "C'mon, Charlie. Please be quiet." He wanted to know if Captain James Cook survived the stormy sea.

As the bruises faded and the cuts healed, the boy didn't notice the sunlight stretching longer and the air growing warmer around him. He didn't notice the new weasels being born, and their weasel-parents needing extra food for them.

The monsters came to the Garden City more and more, on their murderous hunts. They seemed to grow bolder, sensing, somehow, that change was coming. Again and again, the tower bell rang and the Little Ones raced to their secret shelters.

When the all-clear sounded, their little lives went on. Construction crews returned to work on the Great Hall. They had built the walls and the impossible dome was taking form: wood scaffolds held the masons who lay the herringbone brick that vaulted to its peak.

Outside Flestrin's Wall, in a meadow by the cottage, where the clover was ready to bloom, Lem taught Michael to use the old rifle and they practiced on weasel-sized bottles. He showed the boy how to cut back the weeds where the vermin might breed. He passed on every possible trick to keep the Little Ones safe from the dangers of a wide and heartless world.

On a warm morning in March, a coat of waterproofing beeswax was spread on the roof tiles and the Great Hall was finished. Burra Dryth's dream was now real and stood twice as tall as any building in the city. Its fresh-cut stone shimmered in the sun as its flowing walls and windows rose to the startling dome. The main chamber was decorated with mural and mosaics and held the locked vault of the Inevitable MaGuffin. There was a celebration that afternoon, with speeches made and essays read by school-children. There was dancing and singing to the ever-same, never-same tune.

Philament Phlopp had been working for weeks on a new fireworks display. As the night fell, the show began and rockets painted delicate pictures—brief sparkling scenes from the history of their Nation—on the dark still sky.

Michael leaned close when Burton Topgallant said: "Look at this little monster." He was holding something, pinched between thumb and forefinger, but Michael couldn't see anything.

"What is it?" the boy asked.

Topgallant put the thing in a small jar and gave it to Michael. And still the boy could see nothing. "It's what our scientists call a *flflfl*," the G.P. explained. "It's not often you see one."

Michael peered into the tiny glass. "I still don't see one."

"A *flflfl*," Topgallant went on, "is a flea that lives on the back of a flea of a flea. They're really very small."

"Yes," the boy nodded. "Really."

"And yet, it doesn't hesitate to bite me. Imagine! It has no sense of its smallness," Topgallant said as he took back the jar and let the unseen creature go. "Just as it has no sense of my BIGNESS."

From across the Garden City, the tower bell began a sudden pealing. A weasel had slipped over the Wall.

♦ ♦ ♦ ♦ ♦

Lemuel came from the cottage and handed Michael the old rifle and said, "You better take care of that."

And the boy said, "Why me?"

This was the day of Vernal Equinox, when the world reaches its own crossroads and seasons change. On this day, light and dark are equal. On this day and no other, it is said, you can balance an egg on its pointy end.

"Why not you? It's your time." The old man started away. "Besides, I have to go now. I can't say when, or if, I'll be back."

The bell was clanging, louder and faster. More weasels were coming.

"Go where?" the boy asked. "What're you talking about?"

"I'm going to find her," Lemuel answered.

"Who, find who?"

"Maya," said Lem as he headed out of the garden.

"Whoa-whoa, hold on," called the boy. "You're kidding me, right? This is a joke. You're not leaving me here all alone, are you?"

PART TWO

◆

ADRIFT

◆

CHAPTER TWELVE

◆

WHERE ALL ARE KNAVES

But he was. He was going. He was gone.

And the weasels were coming. They were swarming Lesser Lilliput and filling the streets with panic.

The boy took aim and fired and the first shots went wild, one taking out a corner of the church spire. It took half an hour to chase all the vermin from the Garden City.

Michael ran to the stone cottage, but Lemuel and the dog were gone. The boy checked every room, ran to the gravel drive, rode his bike to the crossroad. But they had vanished. In every way, and forever, they had vanished into thin air. It was as simple as that.

Had the old man been planning this all along? Was he just waiting till Michael was ready?

And how would the boy tell the Little Ones?

He knew they were a resilient People. *They can deal with it.* Michael told them the truth. He told them, "Quinbus Flestrin is gone."

And the town exploded in riot. The Little Ones wailed and screamed and some darted around in their underwear. Wagons were toppled, set afire, store windows smashed, and there was a brief run on the bank.

Well, Michael thought to himself, *that could've gone better.*

It took him hours to get them calmed down. He promised he'd watch over them, would check on them every day, would keep them safe, as Lemuel had.

But by the second day, he knew this wouldn't be easy.

He was clearing the drains when he raked open a writhing new nest of weasels, right there in the back garden. Hissing and screeching, the things scattered up and over the Wall, and Michael found the bottom of the nest littered with the tiny remnants of roast rib and leg of lamb and an empty tin of Uncle Joe's Mint Balls, leftovers from Hoggish Butz' many picnics.

When Topgallant asked the People to take better care with their refuse, so not to tempt Monsters from Beyond, Hoggish exploded in a red-faced rage: "What did I hear? Did I hear what I heard?! Is he blaming us?! Is he actually blaming *US*?!"

His big belly trembled, his whole body quivering with anger. "It's *YOUR* job to keep us safe!"

Brother Evet could take no more. "Leave him be. You're the one who's always lookin' to blame somebody."

Hoggish spun on his smaller twin and his great gut tremored. "You! Ha! Like you have any right to talk! The way you *ANTAGONIZE* the poor creatures, shooting your gun at them, you beast! Is it any wonder they're upset!?"

"Ahhhhh, rattletraps," Evet grunted. "I'm the farmer who grows the food to fill your bottomless gullet. I have every right to protect myself. You're the one who brings 'em here."

"Great Ghost of Bolgolam!" Hoggish hollered, hysterical. "Why do I even listen to this slander!? I'm a gentle, peace-loving soul who takes lovely picnics by the lake and ponders the meaning of meaning. I am as *BLAMELESS* as a newborn babe!"

"Now, boys," said the Grand Panjandrum. "We can't change the nature of these monsters. They are only interested in food and we must keep ourselves off the menu."

"And if that means shootin' 'em, we shoot!" added Evet.

Hoggish sputtered and spewed and waved a thick finger at the crowd: "Do you hear that?! They're trying to scare you! Both of them! This is how they plan to control you! With *FEAR!*" And he stormed away, wailing, "Oh, remove me from this land of slaves, where all are fools and all are *KNAVES!*"

There were mumbles, there were grumbles. Some of the People saw Hoggish's point and some saw Evet's side and neither had much use for the other.

Michael had never known them to act this way, so angry with each other, and he had no idea what to do about it. But he knew he had to keep them safe from the peril that filled their small world.

He set his alarm for four thirty each day and left the flat while Freddie still slept. He rode his bike through the wind-whipped mist and reached the stone cottage before dawn. He made his rounds of the little Nation and saw that the People were safe. At seven thirty, he was back on his bike and at school as the last bell rang. Each afternoon, he finished at Fenn's Market and bicycled to the Garden City. After that and check-in with the Court, he was home and in bed.

It wasn't an easy schedule.

On Tuesday as on Monday, he left Fenn's Market and set out for the cottage. But as he reached the crossroads, he sensed that something was different, something was wrong. He pulled to a stop and he saw.

A quarter mile behind him.

A pale yellow car.

Following him.

He stopped.

The car stopped.

It was too far back and Michael couldn't see who was driving. But he *would not* lead them to the cottage, *would not* give away the ancient secrets of Lesser Lilliput. He turned right at the crossroads, away from Lemuel's house, and the car went with him.

He stayed on the farm road and the yellow car followed and they left Moss-on-Stone together.

At about this same time, Father Drapier walked into the village for dinner. Robby and Peter and Phil pried a small gravestone from the ground and smashed the refectory door with it. They crawled into the old church and stole whatever was worth stealing. The rest, they left in shattered pieces.

The sun was fading when Michael reached the next town, Ambridge. He stopped near an Indian restaurant and a coin dealer's shop. Edgy, antsy, and dripping with sweat, he pretended to look in the long window of coins as he slipped glances up the street. The car was parked a half-block away, engine off, lights out. Michael still couldn't see who was in it, but it had to be someone from Youth Court, keeping track of him.

From inside the coin shop, a wary and balding young man squinted at the boy beyond his window.

As soon as a moonless dark took the town and the streets grew shadowed, Michael jumped on his bike and sped off. The car tried to follow on the narrow knotted lanes. But a block ahead, the street was closed for a festival and the boy got away.

He pedaled through the windy night, as fast as he could, the full fifteen miles to the crossroads. Every part of him ached, inside and out, as he stopped to look for the car. He saw no lights, heard no motor. He was alone and safe and he started for the stone cottage.

Michael made a careful check of the Garden City. The Little Ones were well and not a weasel to be found. Dead tired and muscles cramped, he lay in the still-warm clover to rest. There was a concert in the town square that night and the orchestra played Maya's music, loud and soft and soothing. The boy closed his eyes and sleep was quickly on him.

In a little house near the pastry shop, Hoggish Butz was eating a third éclair and listening to Ethickless Knitbone: "Everything is moving as we planned. The others are beginning to question Topgallant, I've heard them. They're starting to wonder if he's all they thought he was, starting to question whether he knows what he's doing. It's time for the next step."

"Ooooo, yessss, the next step, of course!" Hoggish giggled, gurgled. "And what . . . is the next step?"

"We shall call for an election."

"Oooooo, and I, Hoggish Butz, shall run for Grand Panjandrum!"

"Yes, Hoggish," said Knitbone. "And no, Hoggish."

"No, Dr. Knitbone? And yes?"

"You will not run *for* office. You will run *against* Burton Topgallant," she went on.

"Ah, yes, of course. And is there a . . . difference?" he asked softly, unnerved by his own ignorance.

"Immense! You should know this, Hoggish."

"Of course! I'm a clever freethinker, you'll remember. I only thought you might state it the way you see it, to be certain *YOU* have it just right."

She nodded. "To win an election, you destroy your rival. You rob him of all credibility, integrity, dignity."

"Yes," Hoggish nodded thoughtfully. "I'd say you have it about right."

Knitbone took him by the hand and led him to her office, where she had set up a strange machine, old and dark and oily. Hoggish shivered at the sight of it. "Great Ghost of Bolgolam, what's that awful thing?"

"It is the key," she told him, "which will unlock the Hearts and Minds of your Countrymen."

"I never saw such a key as that," he said, taking a few steps back from the foul-smelling heap.

"It's a printing press, you—! A press, Hoggish, for printing."

"Ahhh," said Hoggish, taking a bite of another éclair he'd stuffed in his coat pocket. "I see," he said, though he didn't at all.

"Put down the éclair, Hoggish, and listen to me. Information is Knowledge and Knowledge is Power and Power is Truth and Truth is what the Teller says it is. Do you understand?"

"Except the part after 'Put down the éclair, Hoggish.' Could you repeat that last bit?"

But Knitbone knew it was faster to show him. She began writing scandalous tracts about Burton Topgallant, terrible lies about his hygiene, diet, hairstyle, pets, and grandparents. Hoggish's jaw hung loose at the words he read. "Is— is— is this true?"

"That's beside the point!" she snapped and his eyes grew red and wet with tears. "Listen to me, Hoggish," she went on, kinder, gentler. "What matters is this. He will have to deny these things and the People will ask themselves, 'What sort of a man is it who must defend himself from such rumors?' You see how this works, Hoggish?"

And Hoggish did see, more or less. "Yes— but— it's immoral, dishonest and unscrupulous. May I please try it now?"

When Michael finally woke, he saw a ruddy glow at land's edge and a mist drifting by. He'd been here the whole night!

He jumped on his bike and started home. When he rounded the last corner, onto the street where he lived, he saw a police car at the block of flats. "Where've you been?!" Freddie screamed.

Michael had missed his check-in. The big policeman had come for him.

"Crud! I asked you *where you been?!*"

CHAPTER THIRTEEN

IN THE HORSE LATITUDES

The church had been robbed that night and Stella and Esther were on the phone at dawn, calling an emergency meeting of the Merchants Watch Committee. "A tragedy," said Stella. "What happened to St. Edwards. A senseless tragedy. That beautiful church, destroyed, for no reason."

"Have they found out who did it, have they, have they?" Frances Froth wanted to know. "Well, have they?"

Tiswas stood at the door, dark and distant.

"The authorities know who's responsible," said Stella solemnly.

"Who who who?"

"Those pernicious little vermin, of course," Stella told her.

"They've already arrested one of them," added Esther somberly.

"Who, who, who did they get?" chirped Frances.

"*That boy*, of course," added Stella.

"I knew it, knew it!"

"What boy?" asked Tiswas.

"The boy who robbed your store, Mr. Tiswas," said Stella.

"That horrid delinquent—Michael Pine," added Esther.

Tiswas grunted, still darker and more distant.

"Seems you'd be happy, Tiswas," said Gadbury. "They caught him. Now they can put him where he belongs."

But Tiswas only grunted again.

Michael had been taken to the police station the morning before and kept in protective custody overnight. At midday, he was brought to the Youth Court. Stanley Ford and Father Drapier sat near the wall, both silent, both solemn. Maxine Bellknap and Horace Ackerby were there, quiet and miserable. Mr. Fenworth, the Duty Solicitor, came running in late.

"All right. Tell us what happened." The Magistrate never looked at the boy.

Michael knew by now that the church had been robbed, vandalized, the pipe organ destroyed, half the stained glass windows shattered. But he couldn't tell them where he'd been, couldn't give away the secret of the Little Ones.

"Mr. Fenworth?" Ackerby's temper was rising. "Would he like to tell me or go straight to jail?"

Fenworth glared hard and Michael said, "I was in Ambridge."

"With who?" Ackerby asked.

"I was alone," the boy answered.

"Of course you were," the Magistrate muttered. "And why were you in Ambridge? Conveniently alone, of course."

There was no good answer to give. "I was just . . . there, I guess."

"Someone must've seen you. Someone who can vouch for you."

Michael had no answer. The courtroom door opened and a clerk stepped to the Magistrates and handed a note, which they passed among themselves.

"Let him in," said Ackerby and the clerk brought Mr. Tiswas to the front. "You have something to share with us?"

"This boy didn't break into the church," said Tiswas.

"How do you know that?"

"I was driving home when I saw him on his bike. Thought he might be up to something, so I followed. I stayed with him a good three hours, 'bout five to eight o'clock, all the way to Ambridge."

"That's over ten miles," said the Magistrate.

"Fifteen," Tiswas told him.

"You're certain? Certain it was him?"

Tiswas said he was and Ackerby said, "Still, the boy missed a check-in and he was warned. I propose a Curfew

Order." He turned to Michael: "That means you'll stay indoors at your flat, between seven o'clock each night and seven each morning. If you break this curfew, I'll send you to YOI, y'unnerstand?"

"Yes. Yes, sir."

The Chief Magistrate got to his feet. "We make the Curfew Order."

It was going to be tough, keeping that curfew. But Michael didn't want to end up in the Young Offenders Institution. When he finished his work at Fenn's, he hurried to check on the Little Ones.

He found them clustered in the streets, reading the latest pamphlet.

"What's going on?" the boy asked Mr. Topgallant.

"If only I knew," the Grand Panjandrum sighed, looking old and weary. "Our society has drifted off its course. The Trade Winds have forsaken us and we are stuck in a doldrums of our own making, caught in Horse Latitudes." Topgallant had read about this in one of Lemuel's books. It was a place feared by sailors, where ships lay trapped by a windless sea. In these latitudes, the water is flat as glass and a ship can be caught for weeks, not moving forward or back. It was Spanish sailors who gave it the name: when their ships lay in the stillness, supplies ran low and drinking water went first. There was nothing left for the horses, and these men cared deeply for their animals. They threw the doomed creatures overboard, weighed down, to save them from more miserable deaths. The superstitious ones know that ghost-horses still haunt these waters.

"When you find yourself in the Horse Latitudes," said the G.P., "there's nothing to do but wait and hope you make it out alive."

That evening, with Michael gone, one of them was on tower watch when a weasel and another, another, another slipped over the eastern wall. The Little One leapt to the rope and sent the alarm belling over the Garden City. The People moved quickly to shelters and the Farmer was ready with his rifle. Evet's aim was steady and the first weasel was dead before it hit the ground. The others scurried, barking to one another, up and over the wall.

But Topgallant knew they'd be back. The hawks he could deal with: there were only a few of those and they hunted when hungry. These monsters were worse; they were ruth-less, toothy things and they killed for the joy of killing, madly murdering anything that wasn't weasel.

I can see myself, Topgallant thought to himself, *fading away peacefully at a very old age. I can see myself bravely going down with a ship at sea. But I will not end up as weasel food!*

The next morning, a Sunday, Michael went to Jane's house and waited under a beech tree across the street. The Mallery home was long and many-gabled, built of the sun-yellow stone, with a half-dozen chimneys scattered along the tile roof. Mountains of marigold bloomed everywhere and ivy grew up the front of the house, spreading as it went like angel wings. Jane came out in a bright Spring dress and waited by the car.

"Oh, no, no, noooo, Michael," she said when he came over. "What are you doing here?"

"I need to talk to you," he said.

"You better go." She took a fast look at the house. "Dad'll be coming any minute. Don't let him see you here, please."

"It's important."

"It's Easter, Michael. We're going to church."

"I'll see you after."

When the house door opened, she said, "Here he comes," but Michael had already gone.

He took a seat in a back pew, in the farthest dim corner. Father Drapier had repaired the church as best he could, but the Boys had worked it over. They'd broken most of the stained glass, and sheets of plywood covered the holes. The great Willis organ had been wrecked beyond fixing, the pipework hammered bent and useless.

Michael watched Jane and her father take seats near the front. The old priest began his Mass and its ancient rhythm made the boy think of the Little Ones' music.

"'*Quem Quaeritas?*' the angels asked. 'Whom seek ye?'"

CHAPTER FOURTEEN

◆

STORKS on the ROOF

When the service was done, Michael found Jane in the nave, alone and apart. Her father was talking business with a local television personality as the boy made his way to Jane's side.

"I need your help," he said.

He let her guide him back into the chapel, empty now.

"Help how, Michael, help with what?" she wanted to know.

"Can't say, exactly," he told her. Their words echoed off the old walls, no matter how softly they spoke.

"What does that mean, exactly? Why can't you say, exactly?"

"Can't, that's all. I need to show you," he said.

He waited for an answer, but she said, "You better get out of here, Michael. If my Dad sees you, mannnn, he's going to—"

"There's nobody but you," he said, he pleaded.

It was another long moment till she told him, "All right."

"Tomorrow? Nine?" The schools were closed that Monday. "Meet me here."

She nodded, she would.

"You want to tell me what it's all about?" she asked.

"I want to. But if I did, you wouldn't believe me. Tomorrow. You'll see then."

"Wasn't sure your Dad'd let you come," he said when they met on the windy steps of St. Edwards. Esther and Stella watered boxed geraniums and watched the children closely. Francis Froth peered at them through the pet shop window. Michael walked Jane down the street, away from the many eyes of the Merchants Watch Committee.

"He thinks I'm at Nicole's house," she told him.

"What if he finds out you're—?"

"Let's don't think about it. Now why don't you tell me what's going on?"

"Come on," he said. "I'll show you."

They set out walking, not talking much. When they came to the crossroads Michael said, "If I told you there's a place up here . . ." he chose words carefully, "like you never imagined, like you never dreamed . . ."

"I guess I'd say take me there," she answered.

He gave her his hand and they walked together.

"Unbelievable," was all Jane could say when she saw the Garden City. "How'd it get here, how long's it been here, how'd you find out about it?"

"Wait," he said. "There's more." He used a stick to tap the church bell and called, "There's somebody you need to meet."

"Who, who're you talking to—" Then she saw. Jane saw the Little Ones come from houses, shelters, every corner of the Nation. They gathered in the new square, one hundred ninety-three of them, all in their best clothes. They stood on the fountain, watched from window ledges, in tree branches, rooftops.

"What are—" she asked quietly, "who are they?"

"They're my friends." Michael told her their story, as much as he knew. "They're vulnerable," he said, "to weasels and Sparrow Hawks."

"Where'd they come from?" she whispered.

"Don't know," he answered. "They're the only ones like them in the world, is what they tell me. Nantwuzzled, that's their word for it." He introduced her to the Grand Panjandrum, his wife, to the Tiddlins, Evet Butz, Thudd Ickens, Philament Phlopp, Mumraffian Rake, Burra Dryth, the rest.

"We will call her Quinbus Ooman," the G.P. announced.

"Means 'the Girl Mountain,'" Michael told her.

"Great Ghost of *BOLGOLAM*," Hoggish shuddered, and left for lunch.

Topgallant declared another New Quinbus Day and the celebrating began. There were dancers, jugglers, food everywhere, and the music, always the music.

And again Jane said, "Unbelievable. I never imagined something like this could exist . . ."

"I guess there are whole other worlds all around us, if we bother to look," Michael said. "The old man watched over them, him and his dog, for I-don't-know-how-long. But they're gone. And you and me are the only ones who know about them."

"And you and me," she said, "are we going to take care of them now?"

CHAPTER FIFTEEN

THE GATHERING CLOUDS OF WAR

In their little flat above the bookstore, Stella and Esther Daniels had the same thought at the same moment.

"The key," Stella began.

"Is knowledge," Esther finished.

"That's right, dear. And knowledge is information," from Stella.

They decided that the Merchants Watch Committee, the MWC they called it, needed more information. With street brawls and children ending up in hospitals, the Merchants had to know what was going on in their little town. A newsletter is what they needed.

They went straight to Larry Tiswas and badgered him into putting one together for them. The Daniels were sure *every* merchant in Moss-on-Stone would want a copy.

Together through those stretching-out Spring days, Michael and Jane watched over the Little Ones. Together, they did their best to keep them safe.

Jane went to the Garden City whenever she could and told her father she was with her school friend. And Michael was there every day, at least twice a day, and was careful to keep the curfew.

They were busy every second, exhausted, exhilarated, and they kept each other going. When Michael was stressed, Jane was serene and her serenity calmed him. When he was scattered, she was focused.

And for his part, Michael had opened a whole new world to her, had shown her a place full of possibilities.

But these were dark days in Lesser Lilliput. The weasels knew the old man and his dog were gone. They came over the Wall one night and killed three of the Farmer's cows, four sheep, a goose. Evet Butz heard the animal cries and ran to the field. But he found only mud and blood and monster-tracks.

The Grand Panjandrum ordered double-watch in the tower, but it didn't stop the beasts. They came back and didn't wait for darkness. They went to the farm and killed more cows, more sheep, a pig, another goose.

It seemed the bell rang every hour. Villagers ran from their homes, young ones to shelters, the rest to fight off the monsters. Armed with tiny guns and arrows, they chased the vermin over the Wall and into the Land of Naught and Nil, where all the bad things came from; but the weasels could not be stopped. Soon the livestock would be gone and the beasts would come looking for the villagers.

It was a warm windy night, some sour smell in the air, as Nick sat in the old Victor, in a puddle of streetlight, and watched his Boys work. The house was big and close to the street. It wasn't empty, but these were desperate times for Nick. Michael was lost to him and the Merchants Watch Committee had all the shops guarded. He'd been seeing the 7-A-M tags around town, Lyall Murphy's work, and he knew he had to do something. He had to take bigger chances on bigger hauls.

That's why he sent his Boys into the house with ivy grown like an angel across it. Robby used a thin jimmy on a first floor window. The bedrooms were upstairs but they ought to find computers, televisions, and the like down here.

"Careful you don't break it," Peter hissed.

"Look, I know what I'm doing," Robby hissed back, but he didn't know this was Jane's house and he didn't know about the new security system. He pushed the jimmy hard and, as the window gave way, alarms and floodlights blasted from every corner.

Mr. Mallery was in Jane's room in seconds: "Are you all right?"

"Yeah, but what"—she was still shaking sleep from her head—"Dad, what's happening?"

Her father was already on the phone and the police were already coming.

Robby ran for the street, but Peter and Phil, addled and afraid, went the wrong way. "Fools!" Nick spat as he cranked the engine. Robby jumped in and they fled into the night and didn't stop till they hit the crossroads.

"If they get Phil, that's two times for him."

"It's three," Nick rumbled back. "And the same for Peter."

"They'll get YOI. Eejits."

The Lesser Lilliputians gathered in the Hall that night. There had been a dozen attacks in the day and panic was taking the city. "What do those monsters want from us?!" one of them cried.

"Breakfast, lunch, and dinner!" called another.

"Now, now. We've faced challenges before," said the Grand Panjandrum, a lonely voice of calm and hope. "We'll overcome this one."

"That's no *ANSWER*!" screeched Hoggish. "We have to understand why these things are mad at us."

"Why? They only care about food, Hoggish, same as you. They only want to eat us!" said the Farmer.

"Evet has a point," some murmured. "And Hoggish has another," some mumbled.

"Ahh, rattletraps!" shouted the Farmer. "Don't listen to that pig! He hates us more'n the monsters do!"

"I hate no one," the big man bellowed. "I am in charity with the world."

"I say we kill 'em all!" Evet yelled.

"A good idea," muttered some.

"*YES, BUT* more will come and take their place!" wailed Hoggish. "If we leave *THEM* alone, they'll leave *US* alone!"

"A good point," mumbled others.

"No buts, no buts, no buts!" cried Evet. "If more of 'em come, we kill those, too! Use your loaf!"

And on it went, each with a piece of the answer, but neither with the answer.

"Simple country dunce," screeched one brother. "Use reason!"

"Great blubberous slab!" screamed the other. "Use a gun!"

"Yes, but—" "No buts!" "Yes, but—" "No buts!"

Half the town sided with Evet, half with Hoggish, and these camps came to be called Yesbutzers and Nobutzers.

"Friends, let's look at this calmly," the G.P. pleaded. "Let's talk it through like rational folk."

"You are not rational folk," screamed Hoggish. "At best you pretend to be rational and some"—a sharp glance at his brother here—"*SOME* pretend better than others."

"We can't let emotions rule," said the Grand Panjandrum. "That will split us in two and leave us half as strong as we were." But his words were lost in a sea of ugly anger.

Hoggish and Knitbone worked through the night at the old printing press, setting each word of each scandalous sentence. With morning, a new truth spread through the streets of Lesser Lilliput: *"NATION IN CIVIL WAR!"*

By the time Michael reached the Garden City, the simmering anger had boiled to blistering rage. The Yesbutzers and Nobutzers had stopped talking and fights were breaking out. The boy had no idea how to stop them and only stood there, helpless, hopeless, and watched.

When the first issue of the MWC Newsletter appeared on Mallery's desk, he thought it was junk that had slipped past the *No Free Newspapers* sticker on his letterbox. He was about to throw it in a bin when he noticed the screaming headline—*STREET GANGS TAKING OVER MOSS-ON-STONE!* He put aside his work and sat to read. He read about break-ins, into cars, houses, the church, the tagging, he read the names of the suspects, and he read the name Michael Pine.

Jane's father kept his calm as he walked into the Chief Magistrate's office.

"Good morning, Mr. Mallery."

"Tell me, Horace, is it true you knew that Michael Pine was part of the break-in at my house?"

"No, no!" Ackerby assured him. "There no evidence he was involved in that."

"But he's in a gang," Mallery went on, "and his gang was responsible?"

"Well. Yes. I suppose. The boy was once part of the—"

"Once? And the other crimes—car break-ins, church vandalism—you let him off for those things?" Mr. Mallery wasn't calm anymore.

"Well, no, you see, he—" Ackerby began.

"No wonder!" The blood was darkening Mallery's face now. "No wonder we've got such crime, when you let criminals go scot-free!" He was yelling and courthouse workers paused at the door to peer in. "I'm not safe in my own house, because of you! If something isn't done, Ackerby, you'll be off the bench, I'll make sure of it!"

And he left, still mumbling his anger.

Here was Ackerby's great fear, come true. The voice of the people, rising against *him*. If things didn't change, he'd be out of a job.

The Lesser Lilliputians didn't want Civil War, but the pamphlets said there was one, so there had to be. The Farmer's followers gathered in a fresh field of wheat, a hundred pair of feet grinding the seedlings to pulp. The other army met outside the bakery where Hoggish was picking up battle-field supplies.

The first shot was fired by the Nobutz Army at 1:07 PM and the second went un-fired for another two hours. There was only one cannon and they had to take turns shooting at each other. A swab-pole soaked in water had to be run down the bronze bore to dampen the barrel. Gunpowder, from Mr. Phlopp's fireworks, was shoveled in and a plug of cloth and straw was ramrodded over it. The cannonball was loaded and pushed tight against the wadding.

Evet Butz set a match to the touchhole and the missile went flying, entirely off-target, smashing a hole through the wall of his own farmhouse, wrecking a jigsaw puzzle he'd been working on for months.

"Ahhh, rattletraps."

The Yesbutzers had no better luck: the cannonfire gave Hoggish a Tension Headache—"Great Ghost of *BOLGOLAM*!"—and he ordered his soldiers to use half the gunpowder. And so the next shot made it halfway to the Nobutzer line.

And the battle went on, slowly, for day after day. And each day, the armies fought to a draw. No one was hurt, no one was helped, and it seemed the war might go on without end.

Nick Bottoms found himself in a doldrums. Gordy and Peter and Phil were gone, locked away at the YOI, and Lyall

Murphy's Gang had taken over Moss-on-Stone. One afternoon, Nick went to see Robby.

"We're going to call out Lyall Murphy."

"Who, why?" Robby was sure he hadn't heard right.

"You and me. We'll fight 'em, we'll run 'em off."

"Have you lost it, Nick?" Robby asked him. "You and me are going to fight seven guys?"

"We have to do *something*."

Robby was quiet for a second, then he said, "Listen, Nick. I've been meanin' to tell you. Lyall's Gang asked me to join 'em."

"And you said no." Nick couldn't believe things had gotten so bad, so fast.

"Told 'em I'd think about it," said Robby.

"*You flat-out fool!*"

"C'mon, Nick, I got to do somethin' with my life. Let's be real. The Boys are done with. You should talk to 'em, too."

"My gang's had a setback," Nick grumbled, "that's all."

"You call this a setback? You can't have a gang with nobody in it. You and me. That's not a gang. That's a couple of guys talking."

"We'll get Michael back with us," said Nick. "We'll start over."

"Who? Pine? He's useless! You think you can count on him for *anything*?"

CHAPTER SIXTEEN

AND THE WATERS PREVAILED

When Michael showed Jane what the Lesser Lilliputians had done—when she saw their battle-torn Nation, the scarred land, the shattered buildings—her heart dropped inside her. "Why are they doing this?" she wanted to know. "Why are they acting this way?"

"I wish I knew," was all the answer he had.

The fighting was flaring again, right under their noses, a skirmish in the Farmer's barley field.

"We could give them a time-out," Jane finally said. "Dad used to do that to me when I was little."

"We could give it a try, I guess," said Michael.

And they tried it. The Yesbutzers and Nobutzers were told to sit quietly for ten minutes, on either side of the country, and think about what they'd done.

With the armies in time-out, Michael and Jane started cleaning up the little town. They swept away the broken glass and splintered wood.

"Taking care of them," said Michael, "is more work than I figured."

"We can do it," Jane told him.

The little clock tower struck four and the time-out was over and the fighting started once more.

"We can't give up," said Jane. "That's not a choice we have."

In Moss-on-Stone, Mr. Mallery was running up the stairs and into his office to reach the ringing phone.

"Is Jane there?" A child's voice. Her school friend.

"Who is this?"

"Me. Do you know where she is? I only tried her like two million times."

"Who is this?" Mr. Mallery asked again.

"Nicole. I've called so many times you wouldn't believe. Where is she?"

"I'll tell her to call you," said Mallery.

"Right, tell her call Nicole. Mannnn, she's *never* around anymore, is she?"

And he hung up.

◆ ◆ ◆ ◆ ◆

When she came in that night, Jane found her father in a very dark mood.

"Where've you been?" he asked.

"I was—" But he already knew, she could tell that. "Was with Michael," she told him. "He needed me to help him. It was important."

The fact was this. Julien Mallery hadn't got on well with his parents. The fact was, they were childish people who never grew up. He had wanted to get along with Jane, had wanted it very much. It hurt him that she lied.

She waited, wordless, until he said, "You're a little old for time-outs."

She nodded. "And they don't really work."

"Let's say you're grounded. For a month, I think. Yeah. A month."

Without Jane's help, Michael lost all control of the Lesser Lilliputians. The Civil War raged on and grew worse with each day. Its damage was awful and everlasting. The Grand Panjandrum could have done more, should have done more to stop the fighting. But he didn't.

The war might not have ended, but for what happened early on a Summer morning. Michael had been working hard, too hard, between his job at the Market and the Little Ones and their bickering. He woke with a fever, sweating, shaking, miserable, and couldn't get out of bed.

Billowing black clouds covered the whole county. By midday, thunder was rumbling in like an army on the march, promising a long ugly storm. Ice-white veins of lightning pulsed in the darkening sky. And in Lesser Lilliput, a wind began to blow across the city, for the very first time.

Rain fell through that day and the next, and for a full week, without pause. Before long, the drains of the Garden City were filling with leaves and sticks and every kind of rubbish. With Michael sick at home and Jane grounded, no one had kept the grates cleared. The Lesser Lilliputians might have done it themselves, but they were too busy fighting. The drains were useless now and a flood was rising.

The low meadows were first to vanish: the Farmer's fields of wheat and barley turned to marsh, then lake. Evet moved his grazing livestock through the hard rain to higher, drier ground. By the next nightfall, water lapped at his piggery and some outbuildings were half-underwater. Mr. Butz herded his animals to town and into the Great Hall, making a loud smelly barn of it.

With dawn, the People found water at the outskirts of their own neighborhoods, squeezing tighter like a giant noose. Whole houses were sinking into the flood, chairs, tables, clothes, art, books, fortunes, memories, all washing away and nothing spared. A sailboat from the once-little lake drifted in the street outside Philament Phlopp's work-shop. More and still more of the Little Ones fled to the safety of the Great Hall, packed alongside cows, sheep, horses, geese and pigs.

And the Civil War was forgotten.

None of them had ever seen a storm like this. It struck hard at the little city, merciless and endless, breaking roof tiles and ripping wood siding from houses. Each street was a river now. Everyone looked to the Grand Panjandrum for answers, but he had none to give.

He told his wife, Docksey, not to worry, these were a resilient People and they would take care of themselves. But the Lesser Lilliputians had panicked, completely, and needed someone to guide them.

It was the moment Hoggish Butz had been waiting for and he didn't even know it. Ethickless Knitbone hurried to tell him and found him eating his second lunch of the day.

"Hoggish!" she hissed. "What do you think you're doing?"

"I think I am eating, dear Dr. Knitbone," he said around a lump of suet pudding.

"But my plan! Our plan!"

"Oh, what's the point," Hoggish grunted and waved a sausage toward the storm. "This weather has ended our lovely little *WAR*. Really, dear, what's the point anymore?"

Knitbone had no time for this. Topgallant's inaction, she said, was a greater gift than they could have hoped for.

"What are you talking about?" asked Hoggish. "And pass me one of those spicy buns while you're explaining."

"Burton Topgallant has done nothing to stop the flood," she hissed. "He has given us a serious crisis and we cannot let it go to waste!"

She grabbed him by his fleshy arm and he squealed like a colicky baby. She ignored the cries and pulled him through the rain to her office. They had to make sure that every man, woman, and child knew how useless the Grand Panjandrum really was.

At this same time, across town, two of the Little Ones, Chizzom Bannut and Gulkin Afterclap, found the drifting sailboat and went rowing out to look at the drains. They passed chimney pots and treetops and guessed where the first grate was. The rain was cold and the floodwater colder, but Bannut dove and tried clearing the drains by hand. He found them blocked with a tight weave of branches, leaves and dirt, and held by the weight of a fast-rising sea. The men started rowing back to share the grim news.

Floodwaters encircled the town square, once the highest point in Lesser Lilliput, now a fast-shrinking island. Most of the population had gathered in the Great Hall; Topgallant's own house was gone.

When Bannut and Afterclap told what they'd seen, the rowdy room went silent: they understood that their city was doomed, another Atlantis lost to the world forever. And they would go under with it.

But Philament Phlopp wasn't so sure. An idea was taking root, somewhere deep in his brain. For an hour or more, he kept it to himself and let it grow. As the waters prevailed over their Nation, he began to believe, to *know* that his scheme was their one best chance.

"We must tear down the Wall," he said suddenly, unexpectedly, and a still-greater hush took the Hall.

There were some coughs, some clearing of throats, but the People were too stunned to do more. The Grand Panjandrum said, at long last, "Um. Ah. What was that again, Brother Phlopp? The wall? Which wall are we talking about?"

"Flestrin's Wall," he said. "We have to break through it, so the flood can drain out."

No one, not in three hundred long years, had dared think a thought like this. The Wall was *the Wall* and beyond it lay every peril.

"Great Ghost of Bolgolam . . . !" It was Hoggish, with an armload of freshly printed pamphlets. Dr. Knitbone was at his side. "This man's mad, mad, mad! Without the Wall, we *DIE!*"

For once, most of them agreed with Hoggish Butz.

"We may die *because* of the Wall," Phlopp went on. "It's holding the floodwater in, making an ocean that will drown us all."

"But, Brother Phlopp," the Grand Panjandrum began again, uncertain, unsure, "what if there's an even-greater ocean beyond? If we break through the Wall, more water might pour in . . ."

There were scattered mutterings from the crowd. "Topgallant's right." "We don't know what's out there." "The Wall's been there since the days of my grandfather's grandfather's grandfather."

"Quinbus Ninneter comes from beyond the Wall," said Phlopp, "and Quinbus Ooman, too. It can't all be ocean out there."

There was a long silence then.

"But the monsters," said Evet at last. "You open a path to the Land of Naught and Nil, you'll let 'em in to eat us!"

"All we know," said Mr. Phlopp, "is we have to do something, or there'll be nothing left of us."

The Grand Panjandrum walked to a window and looked out, long and hard, on the storm. "This rain isn't stopping," he finally said, "and the water's getting higher. If no one has a better idea, I say we try Phlopp's way."

There was another long dismal silence and they considered the bad options left to them. Hoggish and Evet Butz and a few others were set against it.

"We couldn't do it if we wanted to," said Evet. "The Wall was built to keep us safe, it was made to be forever."

And that, they all knew, was also true.

"We could do it," a new voice now, Burra Dryth's voice, "if we worked *with* each other, instead of *against* each other." She laid out a plan and it was this:

They would float a raft out to a section of wall where the stones were small and had plenty of cement between them. Using picks and chisels, hammers, drills, they would weaken the old grout and the force of the flood would bring the wall down.

This was her plan and they voted to try it.

And Michael? He was still in bed, sweating through another fever spike. Freddie was in the next room, playing cards with some mates. Jane was at home, still grounded, painting a picture of the Garden City as she remembered it.

The Little Ones worked as fast as they could and built five rafts—huge, by their scale—from trees they found floating, from the timbers of wrecked buildings, the wood siding of houses. Others scavenged the flooded city for tools, picks, sledgehammers, all else. By mid-day, the armada was ready to sail. Each raft held a dozen or so, and twice that number had volunteered. With makeshift oars and poles, they set off down the river-streets and into the still-rising sea.

Phlopp and Dryth found a place where the Wall was weather-worn and built of smaller stones. The rafts were anchored here and they set to work. With picks and hammers and shovels, they attacked the aged mortar. Even in the ruthless rain, the tools sent sparks flying and filled the air with a sour smell.

They worked for hour after hour, but made little progress. A few stones chipped, some cement broke away, but the Wall remained. The Lesser Lilliputians kept at it, even as they understood—silently and all at once—that the whole thing was futile.

But Burra Dryth knew it wasn't. She could see that the Wall was weakening. She told Phlopp that a well-aimed cannon blast might bring the whole thing down.

A few of them rowed back to the Great Hall and loaded the cannon on a smaller raft and strapped it tight. Topgallant called for the workers to abandon their work and return to the city square.

With the cannon-raft anchored a few feet from the Wall, Phlopp fashioned as long a fuse as he could. "I'll wait till everyone's cleared away," he told them, "in case something goes wrong."

"No offense, Brother Phlopp," from Thudd Ickens. "But you better let me, *in case*. I'm the better swimmer."

"He's right," said the Grand Panjandrum. "No one swims like Mr. Ickens."

And they all knew it.

Phlopp left the raft and Ickens climbed aboard and the others rowed off into the flood. He waited until they were a good distance away, then tried to light the fuse. But his hands shook from nerves and cold, and the flint was rain-damp. Ickens tried to calm himself, tried to shake off the sense that something just wasn't right. He struck at the flint again, and a spark jumped to the primed fuse.

And something did go wrong.

The fuse burned in a flash and there was no time for Ickens to get away. The cannon fired a half-second later.

The blast's recoil capsized the raft and sent Thudd Ickens flying into the air, a dozen feet up and then down into the icy sea. The blast hit the Wall squarely and shards of stone and mortar exploded from it. Ickens sputtered to the surface, but dove back to safety as debris began falling with the rain. He came up again, coughing, confused, unsure which way to swim. The downpour was so heavy, it blurred the world and he couldn't tell what was lake and what wasn't. He was blind and lost, until he heard the others yelling to him: "This way!" "Over here!"

When he finally saw the boat, he went swimming toward it and was still a half-dozen feet away when Topgallant told him, "It hasn't worked, Brother Ickens. The Wall's still standing."

But Ickens said, "Don't be too sure, Mr. Topgallant."

He had felt a strong pull at his feet, a sharp new current in the sea. It grew by the second, slowly drawing him back and away from the men in the boat. Philament Phlopp saw hundreds of eddies break across the water surface and he, too, understood what was going on.

"Swim, Ickens, swim!" cried Phlopp.

A fracture had opened somewhere in the Wall, unseen, below the water surface, and the flood was beginning to drain. Thudd Ickens swam with all his strength and then some. But the water was roiling under him and pulling him to the Wall.

What happened next seemed to happen very slowly.

Phlopp held out a makeshift oar and Ickens fought his way to it. They had only hauled him aboard when Topgallant saw a wide section of Wall tremble and collapse on itself. Stones fell loose of the old cement and crashed into the churning flood, falling like a shower of meteors.

The water silently buckled, then raced to fill the new void in the Wall. The boat was dragged with the flood and the men fought to row against it. But it was a lost battle and the surge was sending them to oblivion.

It's fact that Lesser Lilliputians are clever, but they aren't good at thinking ahead. If they had considered the consequences, they might have seen this coming. But they hadn't and now they were being pulled to their deaths in the violent flow.

A moment before the men and their boat would shatter in the rocky rapids, an old tree appeared from the dropping flood. At the last impossible second, Ickens threw a rope and snagged the steady trunk. He pulled them to it, heaving, ho'ing, his hands blistering, bleeding. The men jumped to safety in the tree branches, as their little boat was torn plank from plank and tossed over a monstrous waterfall.

In later days, as Burton Topgallant told the story, Mr. Ickens' daring feat became the stuff of legend. He was the

Hero all children dreamed of being, the one true measure of greatness. "Your daughter swims like Thudd Ickens!" Or, "He's as fast as Thudd Ickens." "Thudd Ickens, you say!" It's something you'll still hear today, now and again.

Back in the heart of the village, they knew the plan had worked: the flood was dropping. More and still more of their wonderful city rose from the sea, shimmering in mud, like a Phoenix, reborn.

In another half-hour, the rain still falling, but lighter, Topgallant, Phlopp, Ickens, and Dryth returned and the Lesser Lilliputians danced the muddy streets and played their eternal symphony on damp instruments. The Farmer, alone, didn't join the celebration: he was too saddened by the loss of that fine cannon.

The storm was not done. In Moss-on-Stone, rain washed the roofs clean and, for the first time in centuries, the River Stone began to flow.

With Michael still sick and in bed, Fenn understood how much the boy meant. He'd made his job easier, had made the market run better, had made it all, well, fun again.

"Uncle— Fenn." The worthless lump Myron was calling from the stockroom.

"What is it?" the grocer coughed.

"Better come see for yourself."

He found Myron finishing more peppermint, his chins wet and sticky. "Michael left his schoolbooks here."

"So?" said Fenn. "He'll be back."

Myron shook his head and said, "Better see what's in 'em." He opened two of the books, to pages where twenty pound notes were laid out, neat and flat. "Looks like he's been stealing from you." He opened more pages to more notes. "There must be three hundred and fifty pounds here, total, what he stole."

"You don't— don't know that." Fenn coughed and turned even redder. "This could be anything."

"Yeah, could be," Myron said, shrugged. "If it was my store, I'd make sure." And he waddled from the stockroom. "'Course it's not— my store."

Fenn went to his office and went over the books, checked, double-checked, and checked again. The store was running close to 400 pounds short.

Myron watched from the door. "Now d'you believe me?"

CHAPTER SEVENTEEN

INTO A NEW WORLD

With the store closed and Myron gone, Fenn wandered the unlit aisles all through the lonely night, quietly wondering. There had to be some reason, some explanation for it, had to be something so simple he'd overlooked it.

Outside, the storm went on. And Fenn could find no answers, as hard as he tried.

With morning, he picked up the phone and called Horace Ackerby II.

At this same dawn, a startling blue sky spread over the countryside. The storm had wrung itself dry and drifted to memory. The People of Lesser Lilliput left the Great Hall to learn what was left of their Nation. Hardly speaking a word, they moved down the streets that ran from the heart of the village.

And the flood's cruel mark was everywhere.

Buildings were mud-stained to the eaves and beyond, windows and doors broken in, furniture swept away. Heaps of trees and shattered houses blocked some streets completely. Here and there gutters held a stray sodden treasure: a doll cloaked in mud, an album of ruined photographs.

They followed the Grand Panjandrum through the silent city, tiny feet slurping the muck that shrouded the land. They moved over flattened fields and came to the spot where the Wall had fallen.

A new stone canyon gaped and through it, in the gold morning sun, they saw another world. They saw an alien land of giant forests and a meadow ten thousand times as broad as any they knew.

There was a ridge of stone, boulders by their scale, piled in the bottom of the Wall chasm. Thudd Ickens climbed onto it. He wanted to see more of this place, and yet he didn't; he was fascinated and he was frightened.

"You're crazier than I ever dreamed!" Hoggish screamed. "Come *BACK* here, you great Blefuscudian Lump!"

"Hoggish is right." It was Evet now. "Every kind of monster is waitin' out there, we know that!"

"Do we?" Philament Phlopp had joined Ickens, crawling the slippery trunk of an uprooted tree. "How can we not explore a place like that?" he wondered aloud as he stared through the crumbled Wall, to everything beyond.

"I'll tell you how!" screeched Hoggish. "We won't go because we *WON'T*! As simple as that! It's *FORBIDDEN*. We've known for centuries that we do not cross the Wall! It was built to keep us safe!"

Burton Topgallant, too, had wandered closer. "We've always thought that, haven't we, Brother Butz? But have we ever known why?"

"*TREASON!*" screamed Hoggish and to the rest he said, "Your own Grand Panjandrum—upholder of Justice, ha-ha, that's rich, I say! He questions the Knowledge of the Ancients!"

"We only know," Topgallant said, "that there is much we don't know."

"Ignore the old fool!" Hoggish cried out. "He'll get us all killed."

The G.P. joined Ickens and Phlopp at the new passage, the threshold between Here and There. "No one should come who doesn't wish. It's true we don't know what's out there. Each must decide."

And most of them chose to find out. Most of the Lesser Lilliputians began to climb through the breached Wall and toward the strange new world. Evet and Hoggish and a few others stayed behind.

As they moved across the flood's flotsam and over the shattered Wall, a new land spread around them and drew them into it. Here, nothing was the same. Forests like cathedrals made great canopies above them. Grass grew as high as their houses. Giant insects roamed the still-wet land.

Young Frigary Tiddlin screamed when a mole as big as a cow crawled from the earth beside her. A few of them grabbed twigs, stones, any weapon they could find, but the thing only sniffed blindly a few times and sank back into the soggy soil.

The Lesser Lilliputians came to a broad field of clover, washed clean by the storm, steam clouds rising with a warming sun. It was primeval and pure, as if they'd stepped back to the First Day, to the beginning of time. The land sloped gently here and Burton Topgallant found the highest point. He saw, in an instant, how wide this world really was. It spread around him in each direction and went on to eternity.

Like Mr. Fenn, the Chief Magistrate didn't want to believe the boy had robbed the store. But what other answer was there? Three hundred eighty-nine pounds were hidden in his schoolbooks and three hundred eighty-nine pounds were missing from the market's accounts. Facts are facts and these spoke for themselves.

Horace sat at his desk for a long time, silently staring out the window. The rain was over, the clouds burned away. He asked himself, again and again, when a trust had been shattered as badly as this, can it ever be restored?

CHAPTER EIGHTEEN

A NEW WORLD

Horace Ackerby picked up the phone and made the call and ordered Michael Pine's arrest.

The boy's fever had broken that morning and he woke up aching and wanting to get back to the Garden City. He showered and dressed and was about to go when he heard a new voice from the next room.

"I need to see Michael."

"What's he done now?" Freddie asked.

"Just get him out here, please." It was Stanley Ford.

"You tell me why."

"I have to take him in," the officer said. "He's going to YOI."

"I haven't been paid for the month!"

There was no way Michael could go. He hadn't done anything wrong. He had to get back to the Little Ones.

While Freddie and the officer argued about money, Michael crawled quietly out the bedroom window. There was a quarter-story drop to a garage roof and he landed on hands and knees. He made his way to the alley and climbed to the pavement. He unchained his bike and set off, to the sound of Freddie yelling and pounding the door of his empty room.

He was crossing the Market Square when Robby saw him and started following in a car he'd stolen, keeping a good distance back. "Find out what he does, where he goes, what he's up to," Nick had said and that's what Robby was going to do; and that's *all* he was going to do.

By the time Michael reached the crossroads, he could hear sirens in the valley below. The police were after him once again.

The Lesser Lilliputians, most of them, were still out in the New World, trying to take it all in. Topgallant looked to the sun and said, "About mid-day, I judge it. We can't stay longer or we'll be caught here in the dark. We'll come back in the morning."

The word spread among them, the grand expedition was returning home for now. Philament Phlopp, who had been cataloguing each new discovery, counted that everyone was there.

But everyone wasn't. One was missing.

Upshard Tiddlin suddenly saw that her son was not at her side and said: "Frigary, where's your brother?"

"He *was* here," the young girl answered.

"Slack!" Upshard called. "Slack Tiddlin!" And again. "Slack Tiddlinnnn!"

The others heard the fear in the mother's voice and they heard the silence that answered. Without a word, without a thought, they raced into the forest, through fern, vine and bramble, calling out:

"Slack!" "*Slaaaaaack*!" "SLACK!" "Slack, boy!" "Where are youuuuuuu?!" "Slack Tiddlin!"

"I've found him, he's here!" One of them had seen the boy, far in a meadow, bared to every unknown danger. They screamed for the child, but only frightened him, confused him, and he ran farther into the field.

Mr. Wellup, the nearsighted journalist, was first to go running. Thudd Ickens went next, Slammerkin Dap close behind, and none of them saw the weasels lurking in the weedy undergrowth. There was no tower bell to sound its warning as the first of the monsters darted toward Slack. Ickens leapt and grabbed the boy, and the weasels took Wellup instead. Slammerkin Dap tried beating them back, but it was all too late.

Michael dropped his bicycle by the door and ran through the house to the Garden City. He slid in the foul mud that covered every street, filling the first floors of houses and shops, and he saw that many structures, sheds, barns, even cottages were simply gone. Tiny trees lay fallen, in tangles of muddy root.

The Little Ones, just returned, told him all about the flood. And then Michael saw the Wall.

"What happened here?" he asked them.

"A long story," said Topgallant.

"Then you better start now," said Michael and they told them the whole thing, about the weasels and poor Mr. Wellup.

"We'll have to fix this," he sighed. He tried his best to rebuild the fallen section, stacking huge heavy stones across the chasm; but these only tumbled down, again and again. With wood from the shed, he patched the hole as tightly as he could. Next, he took an old shovel and started clearing muddy streets. He swept, he mopped, scrubbed, sprayed the soupy muck with a garden hose. The Little Ones worked with him, hauling wagonloads of ruined, reeking furniture to the fields for burning.

The work went on for half-a-day and still wasn't finished when they heard a hammering at the cottage door. "Open up! I know you're in there!"

It was Officer Ford. He had seen Michael's bike.

"What's going on?" asked Topgallant.

"Another long story," the boy answered. "And I don't think it's going to have a happy ending." He knelt by Burra

Dryth and told her Jane's phone number: "Can you remember it?"

Burra nodded, she could.

"She—Quinbus Ooman will be your Guardian for now. Call her if you need help."

The pounding was louder, angrier. Michael told them to get to the shelters and stay there and, "Don't come out till you're sure it's safe."

"Michael!" Ford was in the house.

And the People were safely hidden.

"You've been given a lot of chances, boy." Ford was in the garden now. "And you blew 'em all. Why?"

Michael had no answer.

"Only one course left and that one leads to the YOI. You ready?"

PART THREE

◆

HEAVY SEAS

CHAPTER NINETEEN

YOUNG OFFENDERS

hen you robbed Mr. Fenn's Market," the Chief Magistrate began, with a faraway voice, "you robbed us of hope that a boy like you can change."

Michael gave his word, he hadn't taken any money.

But the Magistrate said, "Facts are not fungible and these facts speak for themselves. We took a chance on you and you let us down." Then he signed the order sending Michael to the YOI in Ambridge.

Michael and another boy were the only ones in the van that night. A wire mesh separated them from the driver, who sang loudly and not well the whole long trip. The other lad, fifteen or so years old, sobbed like a baby all the while.

And Michael watched moonlit farms drift past the window, watched meadows of sleepy sheep sail by, and the spires of other stone villages. He looked out on passing houses where families gathered in bright-lit rooms.

The van was let through a gate in a tall wire fence, and parked by a damp stone building marked Reception. The Young Offenders Institution had been a boys' school a hundred years back and a mass grave for the plague-dead before that. Michael and the weepy teen followed a man to a small room. They waited one slow hour, until a doctor came and looked them over, quickly. A second man came and took their papers and gave them toothbrushes and told them the rules. They were given a pair of jeans and a T-shirt and told to change there.

A guard came next and took Michael, and he never knew what became of the crying boy. They went to a new building, plain, concrete, one story, built around an open court. Michael was put in a cell by himself, and here he found a battered metal desk, a chair, a lamp, pin board. There was a toilet and sink, both brown and chipped. There was a small noisy bed and a thin stained mattress. There was no place that wasn't scratched over with graffiti.

Michael wanted to sleep, but his dreams wouldn't let him.

◆ ◆ ◆ ◆ ◆

The Lesser Lilliputians had done as he asked. They waited to hear the police car crunch down the gravel drive. They waited for silence and then, only then, they came from their shelters.

"You can go back to your homes, what's left of them," the Grand Panjandrum told them. "All is safe." But he couldn't have been more wrong.

Evet Butz went to check on the few cattle he had left and heard a rustling, a scritching, a scratching in the darkening forest past the farm. "Ahhh, rattletraps," he said, a whisper.

Moonlight was fading behind a lone cloud when he saw a shadow move. Something brushed a tree and he caught a glimpse of hungry yellow eyes. Weasel after weasel crawled through Michael's makeshift Wall patch, a whole ghastly army pouring in.

In the city, everyone heard the Farmer's rising cry to, "Run, run, run!" The G.P. saw the monster horde and called the Beacon Tower to sound the alarm. People hurried to battle posts, grabbing what weapons they could. Others ran to the shelters, but most of these were still flooded and filled with mud.

One of them leveled a crossbow and the arrow stopped the beat of a weasel heart. It fell where it stood, a surprised look in its ugly eye, but others took its place, climbing over their dead comrade and charging on.

The monsters knew their time had come.

The Grand Panjandrum knew it, too. This was the full-out attack that had haunted him. The Farmer and Postman loaded the cannon as weasels sniffed the village and found the shelters. With carnivore-claws, the rodents dug at hidden hatches and secret doors. Topgallant saw that the hideouts were useless and called, "To the Great Hall! Hurry now, hurry!" It was the only building strong enough to keep the monsters out.

With spears and guns and arrows, a few of them held the weasels back as the People escaped to the muddied Hall. Hoggish Butz was last to waddle in, and just in time. The Lesser Lilliputians shouldered the doors closed, but one of the things pushed through his toothy snout. Topgallant's wife ground out her Rhodesian pipe on the tender nose and the beast drew away with an angry anguished squeal. The doors were shut and bolted.

"They can't get us now," the Grand Panjandrum reassured them, and himself. "The doors are iron and the walls are solid stone."

But the ceiling above was wood, and weasels were gnawing their way in. Slobbery splinters rained on the Little Ones.

"What now!?" wailed Hoggish. "*WHAT NOW*?"

Then, from a distance, a hopeful sound: the small whine of a steam engine. When he first saw the weasel hordes from the distant railyard, the Engineer coupled every possible car to his locomotive and set out for the city's main station. If he could get the People aboard, he was sure he could outrun the beasts.

As he drew closer, the Engineer let go the throttle and quietly pulled the train into the station. He made his way, carefully, through back streets and rapped at the Great Hall's side door. When he'd told Topgallant the plan, they called to the People together: "We're going for a train ride, come on now, single file, no talking, that means you, Frigary Tiddlin."

The Lesser Lilliputians pattered through the muddy side streets and into the station house. The weasels, still gnawing at the Great Hall dome, didn't see their prey slip silently away.

The People were piling into railcars by the time the weasels caught their scent and let out furious barks. The beasts crawled from the Hall and into the station as the Grand Panjandrum made his way along the coaches: "Close the windows, that's it, lock them tight!" Even now, the wretched weasels were smashing through the flood-ravaged station.

The locomotive's drive wheels spun on the mud-slicked track and the Engineer poured extra sand for traction and the train moved off in a steamy fog, its couplings catch-catch-catching. It pulled out of the town center, a fire-bellied serpent, picking up speed, racing for the countryside. But the weasels weren't far behind.

Philament Phlopp knew they'd only bought themselves time and not much. Sooner or later, the beasts would understand that the train was only running in one great circle.

Then Mr. Phlopp began to remember something.

It had been, what, a week, two weeks ago?

Yes, two weeks back.

Before the flood, before the war, he'd been working on a fireworks show to mark the coming of Spring. It would have been the grandest he'd ever attempted: twice the usual rockets, with bigger charges, louder blasts, brighter displays and more—much more—gunpowder. He remembered loading the rockets for delivery to the town center, a delivery by train. If those explosives were part of *this* train . . .

Phlopp made his way down the carriage and into the next, and through one more. The way was blocked then, by a freight wagon. The train had reached top speed by now, swaying side-to-side, ready to fly from the track at any second. Phlopp struggled up the ladder to the car's rocking roof and carefully made his way to a hatch. A fast look was all he needed: it was packed tight, every inch, with fireworks. At least a thousand *rinniks*, a full Lilliputian ton, of gunpowder filled that car.

There was only one thing to do.

Phlopp hurried back to the last three cars and started moving the passengers to the front of the train. He helped them up the ladder, to the top of the wildly rocking freight car. It was a dangerous, risky climb, but there was no choice and all of them did as he asked. As the Lesser Lilliputians moved along the roof, some of them crawling, terrified by the height and speed, the weasels saw and charged faster after them.

As the passenger cars emptied, one after the other, Phlopp uncoupled it. The cars went rolling, slowing, and the weasels stopped to sniff out each one.

When the Lesser Lilliputians were safe in the front-most cars, Phlopp set to work making a long fuse. He waited for the weasels to catch up to the train, not a long wait. He heard the first of them leap to the roof and he moved closer to the door, to the passage between cars. He could hear more and still more of them jumping onto the freight car, chewing its wood-plank roof.

And still he waited, listening to the grinding of their teeth. When one of the monsters chewed through, Phlopp lit the fuse and bolted the door and let the freight wagon loose. He hurried to join the others, as the weasel-crusted car drifted free of the train.

With a lighter load now, the rest of the train pulled away and left the slow-rolling wagon behind. The People gathered at windows to watch, but Phlopp warned them back from the glass.

A second passed and another and then, all at once, the gunpowder exploded. A light as bright as day flooded the coach and the sound of the blast came next and shattered every window in every railcar.

The freight wagon went up in a red riot of flame and train and weasel-parts. The Little Ones cheered and the Engineer let off the throttle as they watched the great fireball roll into the night sky. The weasels were gone from the earth and the People were safe, at least for now.

From his bedroom window, a half-dozen miles away, Nick Bottoms saw the fiery glow and briefly wondered what it was.

That next morning, Michael was taken to the Recreation Room and three voices rang off the cold concrete walls: "Good to see you, squire!" "Knew you'd make it sooner or later!" "You poor swot!"

It was Peter, Gordy, Phil, and they wanted to know about Nick and Robby. Michael told them as little as he could, and let them fill in the rest as they chose.

"You're going to like it here, Mike," Gordy said and seemed to mean it. His face was still red and puffy from the dog bites, but he looked happy.

"If you need anything, squire, just let us know," said Peter.

Michael saw a guard watching and wished the boys would leave him alone.

"We got everything, Mikey, everything! Three meals, billiard room, telly, exercise yard, everything!"

"And all built on a plague pit," Phil added. "Ten thousand peasants, dead from the plague, buried right under our feet."

Michael tried wandering off. But they followed.

"Where're you staying?" Gordy wanted to know.

He waved a hand toward the building at the far corner of the prison yard.

"12-A? You're kidding me!"

Michael shrugged, no.

"They put him in Seg!"

"What's Seg?" the boy asked.

"That's the Segregation Unit, squire," said Peter. "They only put the special ones in 12-A."

"It means you're VP, Mike!" Gordy shouted.

"What's VP?" Michael asked.

"That's a Vulnerable Prisoner." Peter laughed till he nearly choked.

Michael was glad when his time in the yard was done. He was taken back to his cell in Seg and he sat on the foul bed and thought about the Little Ones.

They'd be better off without him, that much was sure. He couldn't take care of himself. What ever made him think he could take care of them?

CHAPTER TWENTY

---◆---

WHERE THE WIND'S ALWAYS BLOWN

Horace Ackerby was at his usual table at Folk-in-the-Clover, looking out on the windy graveyard and thinking, only thinking. As the news about Michael moved through the town, so did the calls for the Chief Magistrate's resignation. He was about to lose his job and all the things he cared about, but he wasn't going to give up his dinner. The wiry cook brought the pig's nose with parsley-and-onion sauce and Horace said:

"I am remembering myself, Bertram, as a little boy, fishing with my father. I feel a strong tug at my line, and another. Quite fierce. I know I've hooked the biggest fish ever to swim the river. I know this in my heart. I see the creature in my mind's eye, a monster, something from a myth, from a lost race of river-giants. They'll put my picture in the paper, I'm sure. I nearly have it reeled in, so close I can see its silver shadow flash under the water! And then . . . then my line drops back, empty and useless. The fish has got free, Bert, it's gone."

And he added:

"My life's been pretty much downhill since."

The cook, not knowing what to say, said nothing and left. Ackerby stared at the food, but his hunger was gone.

He remembered how his Dad began taking him fishing when some schoolmates joined a gang. Ackerby-the-Father wasn't going to see that happen to his son. He took young Horace to football games, went camping with him, made him take piano lessons. It was the music that worked. Horace Ackerby II loved music and spent his spare hours at practice. He and some friends started a band—The Restless Ones, they called themselves—and they were really quite good. True, as he grew, he slowly forgot about music and the piano sits in his home, unused. But there was a day, once, when a band kept him out of a gang.

Horace realized he'd invested more of himself in Michael than he'd imagined. He had thought, had *hoped*, he could keep Michael out of a gang, too. But he'd been let down, absolutely.

Maxine Bellknap, sure the whole thing was her fault, resigned from the court and took her retirement at last. As Ackerby went back to his lonely meals at Folk-in-the-Clover, she went back to her home and let the hours drift away, unused. Her garden went wild: chickweed and dandelion began to fill the flower beds.

Mr. Fenn spent long lonely hours sitting quietly in his office, lost in aimless dreams. The shelves of his store went un-straightened for day after day.

They were still cleaning up in Lesser Lilliput. The weasels had done real damage to the Great Hall—the dome was near collapse—but the G.P. was sure it could be brought back.

"My friends—" he began, when a louder voice drowned out his.

"Friends, you say?" Hoggish was calm and confident this night. He smiled to the smallish crowd. "With friends like him, we don't need enemies, do we?"

"Now, Hoggish," one of them warned, "we don't want another war."

"Exactly!" Hoggish said, clapping and smiling. "That's the *LAST* thing we want."

"If only," added Dr. Ethickless Knitbone, "we had a Grand Panjandrum who could keep the peace *and* keep us safe, from weasels and floods and fires!"

"Precisely," said Hoggish. "Someone bold, decisive, someone like . . ."

"Someone like Hoggish Butz!" called Knitbone, alone in her zeal.

There were mutterings among the crowd: Topgallant *had* been G.P. for a while, hadn't he? Maybe he needed a rest.

The Reader will be spared details of the campaign that followed. But it was a horrible thing. Hoggish and Dr. Knitbone used their printing press to spread horrible rumors about Burton Topgallant and he wasted too much time denying these. They hinted that he wasn't one of them, but *Blefuscudian* by birth. They called him "*nobbulous* and *griffic*," meaning "old and cranky," implying dementia.

A few days later, with each vote counted at least once, Hoggish won the election, 284-191. They said that the cemetery vote put him over the top. In a hasty ceremony, the Golden Helmet was set on Hoggish's head at last.

And what sort of leader was he? How would one define the Grand Panjandrumcy of Hoggish Butz? These questions will be left for some distant historian to answer.

Because his reign lasted only twenty minutes.

As soon as tables had been laid out with Hoggish's beloved éclairs, the coronation began. "Friends, Citizens—!" he bellowed.

But a louder voice drowned out his.

"Look at that, look at them!"

"I beg your pardon, whoever you are," Hoggish sniffed at the crowd. "You're interrupting what's going to be a very good speech. Now, listen and learn. Ahem. Friends, CITIZENS—"

"What *are* those things?" again, the new voice.

"Well, excuse me!" Hoggish was on his feet, red in the face, waving a fat finger. "*WHO* dares speak when the Grand Panjandrum speaks? Don't you see this beautiful Golden Helmet on my head!?"

He happened to look up then. He happened to see Nick Bottoms and Robby towering over the city, like two Colossi.

"Well . . . Great Ghost of *BOLGOLAM*."

Days ago, Robby had tracked Michael here to the stone cottage. Tonight, he had brought Nick.

"You ever seen anything like 'em? What do you figure they are?"

"Must be some sorta Spriggans or Leprechauns, Dobbies," said Nick. "I guess I don't much care. They got to be worth a fortune."

"All right, Panjandrum," Evet Butz turned to his brother. "What do we now?"

Poor Hoggish was speechless and bits of spit dribbled from his open mouth. It was Topgallant who called for everyone to, "Run! Run, Brothers, run, Sisters, run!" And they ran, fast, but Nick and Robby were faster. The giants scooped up one Lesser Lilliputian after another. There was complete, hopeless panic in the Garden City, all of them running and screaming and crying.

The Architect made it to his studio, but Robby kicked out a window and snatched him up. The Accountant hid under his office desk, but Nick smashed the building front and found him. Another of them dashed into her store and locked and chained and blocked the door, but Robby ripped off the roof and got her.

In all the madness, Slack and Frigary Tiddlin were separated from their mother. They'd run to the Farmer's field and Robby saw them there. He went for them, clumsily slipping in mud, crashing through yards, fences, houses, overturning trees, but Thudd Ickens got there first. Much more agile than the Giant, he escaped with the young Tiddlins through the patch in Flestrin's Wall. Burra Dryth, Mumraffian Rake, Philament Phlopp, these few also made it through the wrecked Wall.

Some others reached shelters, but the Giants used picks and shovels to dig them out. Most of Lesser Lilliput was laid to waste and the nightmare ended only when Nick was happy they'd got all of them. The boys stashed the Little Ones in a rubbish bin, boxes, whatever they could find.

"A few of them got away, over the wall," Robby told him.

"They won't last long out there. Something'll eat 'em."

"What're we going to do with these?" Robby wanted to know.

"Let's get 'em back to my house. We'll start spreadin' the word, start building up some interest, right? We'll let everybody know we got something special, something Lyall Murphy will *never* have," said Nick. "We'll split 'em up, they'll bring more that way. We'll sell the squits, one by one, for a million pounds."

At the Wall-edge, Philament Phlopp heard it all.

"These little things are going to make me big," Nick laughed.

The market was closed and dark and still. Fenn sat in his office, with time slowly passing around him. On his desk sat the nearly 400 pounds that Michael had stolen.

Fenn picked up the money and counted it, as he had many times. But tonight, in the stillness and the desk lamp glare, he saw something he hadn't seen. He took a closer look and saw that each of the pound notes was lightly, slightly smudged. Gooey, grubby, chubby-fingered peppermint smudges.

Ickens, Phlopp, the others—refugees of the blitz—gathered in the stone cottage and considered their dismal future.

They needed help.

They needed Quinbus Ooman.

And Burra Dryth had the number.

When they called to tell her what happened, Jane knew she had to get to them, grounded or not. She wrote a note for her father: "Michael needs me—will explain—love—Jane." She grabbed what money she had and hurried to Lemuel's house. The few survivors were waiting on the porch when she got there.

"Do you know where he is?" Jane asked them. "Do you know how to find him?"

CHAPTER TWENTY-ONE

◆

THE KEY TO ALL LOCKS

Fenn went to his brother's house, a run-down Tudorbethan, and asked to see Myron. "In the kitchen," his sister-in-law told him, "having a little snack."

The grocer set the pound notes on the table, smudgiest on top, and Myron looked up from a dish of peppermint ice cream he was sharing with the cat. "Look at that," Fenn said simply. "Three hundred and ninety-eight pounds."

Myron said nothing, but kept eating.

"But you knew that of course."

Myron shrugged and ate.

"Did you count it— before you hid it in his schoolbook?" Fenn asked.

Myron didn't answer.

"You can tell me. I'm not going to kill you," Fenn went on. "I just want to know the truth. I saw how the notes had peppermint on 'em and I thought to myself— nahhh, Myron isn't as clever as that."

Myron grinned. "Oh, I'm as clever as that."

"You set him up. He never stole anything. It was clever little Myron, all along."

"Clever little me," Myron's grin grew wider, "all along."

Fenn grabbed him by the thick throat and started choking him. His mother screamed, the cat squealed, ice cream went flying, and Myron gagged for air. It took both father and mother to pull the son free.

The taxi driver had a stubbly beard and teeth browned from cigarettes. Jane asked him to stop down the block from the YOI gate. She gave him an extra ten and told him he could take her back to Moss-on-Stone in a few minutes. He wanted to know, *What's going on?*, and she told him, *Just wait, please,* and he took her money and waited.

Jane carried her rucksack to the chain-link wall around the lockup. The driver watched her through the mirror. This wasn't the sort of fare he had every day.

Away from the cabdriver's eyes, she helped the Little Ones from the backpack—Ickens, Phlopp, Mumraffian

Rake, Burra Dryth, the Tiddlin children—and begged them to find Michael as quickly as they could. The guard in the Gatehouse saw her and asked what she was doing.

"Nothing," she called back.

"Then go do it somewhere else," he told her.

The Little Ones slipped through the fence and across the dew-damp Recreation Yard. They reached a dark corner of the first housing block, next to the Reception Building, and Slack spotted an open vent in the Chaplaincy. "That's just what we need," said Ickens.

They had nearly made it to the vent when a dog ran at them, a dusk-colored mammoth, snapping and snarling. Jane saw it from the fence and screamed, sure it was the end of them.

"What d'you have over there, Buster?" the guard called. "Find a li'l snack? Rat, weasel, what?"

Slack took a step, straight toward the dog, as the guard left the Gatehouse.

"Slack Tiddlin!" Phlopp yelled, a whisper.

"Settle . . . settle . . . ," the child told the mountainous dog.

And the dog did settle and little Slack moved closer. He began to rub the giant, gently, a spot between ear and eye, and the beast grew calm and peaceful.

The guard stopped. "Got away from you, huh, Buster? Don't worry. The yard is fulla little things for you. Come on back with me."

◆ ◆ ◆ ◆ ◆

When Julien Mallery found his daughter's note later that night, he made three telephone calls. First he called the police, who began a search and sent an alert through the county. The second call went to his friend at the local television station; the newsman got Jane's picture on the air quickly, with a plea for information on her whereabouts. And last, he called Horace Ackerby to say he'd be out of a job in the morning.

But Ackerby didn't answer his phone.

He was on the front walk with Mr. Fenn. "I'll let it ring," he told the grocer as the phone rang and rang inside. "Please. Go on with your story."

And Fenn went on. "When I saw the goo all over the money, I went to my brother's house and had a— had a talk with that brat and I was right. It was the fool Myron did it, tryin' to get the boy fired. Michael never stole a thing."

Horace Ackerby said nothing. It had been a long while since he'd heard good news.

"Michael's got no business in YOI," Fenn went on. "Should be Myron in there. You can get him out?"

"Wilson, the prison governor, has gone home by now," Ackerby answered. "But I'll be in Ambridge in the morning and see to it myself."

Even as he spoke these words, three Lesser Lilliputians were crawling through a battered grate and into the Chaplaincy ductwork. The ventilation system was like a carnival maze, a catacomb, and they had no idea where to turn. "We could spend eternity here," said Mumraffian Rake, "and never find him."

"I have a thought," from Frigary Tiddlin.

She began to sing their one song, the ever-same, never-same song, and its melody drifted through the vent tunnels. The others joined her, whistling, humming, singing, tapping out a rhythm on the walls. Their music grew louder and louder in the endless ducts, echoing through the whole prison.

Plenty of boys heard it, but only Michael knew what it was. He stood on his cell bed, close to a vent, and began to whistle along with the tune.

"I hear him," said Ickens, "down this way," and he led them through a vent-tunnel. Frigary's torch lighted a path, past webs full of dust and the broken husks of long-dead bugs. The Little Ones rounded a junction and found themselves facing a mangy mouse, big as a draft horse by their standards. Thudd Ickens didn't want a fight, but the mouse was more frightened of them and it scampered off into ductwork.

Their journey was almost done now. Michael's song was coming from the next vent, not far ahead.

They crawled through the clover-shaped grille and Michael set each of them on the rank old bed. Burra Dryth explained, in as few words as she could, all that had happened and all that was going to happen. As she spoke, Mumraffian Rake, the little locksmith, made fast work of the cell door. In a matter of seconds, the group was moving down the corridor, under dim portraits of past prison governors. There was one last lock to pick and then they were outside, in the main yard.

Mr. Phlopp easily sabotaged the prison's power lines—it took only a paper clip—and every transformer within five miles went up in showering sparks. The baffled guard ran to the darkened forecourt, as the front gate's lock fell open behind him.

One minute more and Michael was out of the Young Offenders Institute and climbing into the cab. "Jane," he said when he saw her. "How did you—?"

"Just get in," she said and he did. The Little Ones slipped into her rucksack and she told the driver, "You can take us back to Moss-on-Stone."

"How'd you get me out—?" Michael started to ask her.

Jane told him to be quiet and he was. She wanted to tell him everything, but the taxi driver was listening to each word. She gave him a shirt she'd brought, one of her Dad's, to cover the Institute's T-shirt.

The driver watched them in the mirror and finally asked, "What're you two up to? What's going on? Who's the boy?"

"Let us out here," Jane told him when she saw a petrol station and coffee shop.

"You want me to drop you off, two kids, this late at night, middle of nowhere. You said you wanted to go back to Moss-on-Stone."

"Yeah, but I need a toilet," Jane lied and nudged Michael and he lied, too. "And me. Really do. Right now."

The driver grumbled, "*Kids*," and pulled into the station and the children got out of the cab.

"Hold on," the man said. "Maybe I'm going in with you."

Jane took her rucksack and they hurried into the shop. The driver went to the counter and ordered a coffee and waited while Michael and Jane stepped around a corner to the lavatory. They could hear the driver chatting up the counter girl, and they could hear a news report from the small television on the wall, broadcasting a story about Jane: she'd been missing since six o'clock and anyone with information should call the police, right away.

"You see that?" said the driver.

"Been showing her picture all night," the counter girl told him. "Hope they find her, the poor thing."

"She was in my cab," the driver grunted. "And a boy with her, too."

"TV said there's a reward."

The driver was on his feet, fast as that. "They're in your loo right now." He sent the counter girl in to get them.

But they weren't there. When they heard the report, Michael and Jane slipped out a side door and into the night.

"It's empty," the counter girl told him and reached for a phone. "Better call the police."

"No," the driver grumbled. "I'm going to find those kids myself and see I get that reward." And he, too, went into the night.

With the Little Ones still in the backpack, Michael and Jane started down a farm road from Ambridge to Moss-on-Stone. Jane told him what she knew and the Lesser Lilliputians told the rest, about the giants, the wrecked city, the kidnapping of the People.

When they heard a car coming, the children jumped into a wheat field and hid. The taxi passed once, slowly, but the driver never saw them. It was going to be a long walk back and the night wind was cool and getting cooler.

The sun rose behind morning fog as Horace Ackerby II pulled into Ambridge and through the gates of YOI. He met with Governor Wilson at nine and together they found that Michael had escaped.

Ackerby shut his eyes and said nothing. The boy was blameless—hadn't robbed the market—hadn't done a thing—but none of that mattered. Now Michael had committed a serious and unforgivable crime.

Wilson threatened to fire the prison staff then and there. No one, *no one!* had broken out of the Institute during his time as Governor. He wanted to put out an APW, an All Ports Warning, but Ackerby talked him out of it.

When they reached the city, the children kept to alleys and side streets. Michael went for the bike at Fenn's and they made their way to Nick's house.

He remembered the old shed, grown over with weeds and vine. Its door was clear now, and padlocked, and Michael was sure the Little Ones were in there. He found a piece of rusted pipe and, with Jane helping, pried the door off its hinges as softly as they could. They crawled inside, over mountains of junk. "I'll look on this side," Michael whispered. "Check that box over there."

"Just toys," Jane whispered back.

"Nick's stuff, I guess."

"It's dolls," she told him. "Must be his sister's."

"Nick doesn't have a sister."

"Oh," she said. "Well then."

They soon found the Lesser Lilliputians, in the farthest corner, trapped in boxes and bins, huddled together, terrified and terrorized, but unhurt.

"It's okay," Jane told them. "We're going to get you home."

They worked quietly, quickly, and loaded the Little Ones into the bike's delivery baskets and wire-framed trailer. "It's going to be a little cramped," Michael whispered.

"No need to worry about us, Brother Ninneter!" said Topgallant. "We'll get by."

Michael and Jane were ready to go, but, once more, they found their path blocked.

"You trying to steal my Spriggans?" said Nick.

Robby was at his side. "Told you, you couldn't count on him."

"I tried to help you, Michael," Nick seemed mad and hurt at the same time, "but you always thought you were better than us. I tried to show you the way, but you never listened."

When he was younger, Michael thought Nick's gang was the family he was seeking. Now he looked again and saw wasted lives. "I guess my way went somewhere else."

There was something new in Michael's voice, and Nick heard it. There was a confidence, a certainty, a BIGNESS that hadn't been there before.

"You're not going anywhere," from Robby.

"Out of the way, you Blefuscudian Lump."

"What'd he call me?" Robby asked, just as Michael threw himself at them.

He caught Robby by surprise and they both fell to the gravel. While Robby was catching his breath, Michael punched Nick once in the face and felt a tooth break. Jane grabbed the rusty pipe and started swinging.

Nick and Robby backed away, and Michael told Jane to run. As she went for the street, he leapt onto the bike.

"You can't have 'em!" Nick cried out. "They're mine!"

Robby started off, but Nick held him back and spat out a mouthful of blood and tooth and said, "We'll take my Dad's car."

Nick gunned the old Victor and Robby said, "I'm going to beat that eejit to a pulp. I'll show him who's a lump."

Michael was flying up Grub Street when he heard the car tear around a corner. He turned the bike, fast, and nearly went down, the trailer close to tipping, and he yelled to the Lesser Lilliputians, "Hold tight!" Nick and Robby and the Victor were almost on him and there was no way to outrun them. He might have a chance if he got one more block, but the car was barreling at him.

He jumped the bike onto the walk and the car stayed with him, smashing street signs as it went. They passed the Daniels' bookshop, Tiswas Electric, and the Victor blasted through Gadbury's sidewalk display. A chair, plow, clock, boxes of magazines flew into shattered shreds.

The car was going to run him down, but there was another turn, a few feet farther, and Michael made it a half-second before the Victor would have hit him.

Nick jammed the brake and the car slid to a stop in a blue fog. He reversed, full speed, and made the turn. Michael was halfway down the block now and Nick had the accelerator flat to the floor. The old Victor was going 45, 50, 55 mph, before Robby saw where they were.

"Sheep Street, Nick, it's Sheep Street!" But it was too late.

The brick walls closed in on them and squeezed the car, and sparks showered in the narrowing roadway. The old Victor hurtled to a stop, crumpled and stuck.

Michael headed on in the morning mist.

Every policeman in the village showed up on Sheep Street. Jane waited until it was safe, then slipped through alleys and out toward the countryside. It took the Fire Department two hours to get Nick and Robby out of the wrecked, wedged car.

That afternoon at Youth Court, Horace Ackerby asked, "Why did you try to drive a car down a street built for sheep?" He took off his glasses and rubbed his tired eyes and waited.

"Had to get my Spriggans back," Nick answered.

"Spriggans," the Chief Magistrate said and said it again. "Spriggans. As in little people."

"They were stole from us," chimed Robby. "Those things were ours."

Ackerby adjourned the Court and Dr. Emmanuel Kirleus was brought in to evaluate Robby and Nick. A week later, he would present his professional conclusions.

"After careful observation," Kirleus began, "I can say that a traumatic event has led to these delusions. Sensations of panic have caused the break from reality and the young man now sees Leprechauns—"

"Spriggans," said Nick.

"These Little Folk are only projections of his own small-ness, his own inadequacy. The other boy, the weaker per-sonality, has accepted the fantasies as real."

"Hey, hold on." Robby this time. "Is this eejit saying we're nuts?"

The two of them were sent to YOI, for a long while, with recommendations for intense counseling.

When they met in Lesser Lilliput, Michael, Jane, and the Little Ones got a good first look at the wrecked Garden City. There was nothing untouched or undamaged by Robby or Nick, the war, the weasels, the flood. The People went to check on houses, shops, and found everything in ruin. The Tiddlin children crawled through rubble to their old rooms; Philament Phlopp's workshop was collapsed and he had to look away.

When the Librarian saw ten thousand books scattered across the ground, she began to cry. The shoe shop was no more than a pile of bricks. The buildings of the Mount Oontitump University lay flattened and the dome of their Great Hall had collapsed.

Chizzom Bannut, Burra Dryth, Mumraffian Rake, no one's home had been spared the violence. Burton Topgallant walked the shattered streets and knew that his Nation would never again be what it had been. He began to wonder if, maybe, this had to happen. Maybe they'd grown self-centered and small. Maybe, if they started over, they could get back to things that had made them a great People. Maybe they could become even greater.

Suddenly, Michael turned and started running.

"Where are you going?" Jane called, but he was gone.

He broke into the locked stone cottage and searched through boxes that he and Lemuel had packed.

"What are you looking for?" Jane was beside him now.

"A key," he told her, "that opens all locks."

A few minutes later, with all the Little Ones gathered close, Michael slid the dark key into the muddy vault and turned it, carefully. The barrels clicked and the latch popped open.

The boy lifted the lid, gently, and there it was, untouched by weather or war. There was the First & Only Secret, the Solution to the Infinite Enigma, the Unraveling of the Eternal Conundrum, the Resolution to the Ever-Lasting Riddle, the One Answer to All Questions.

"Well, Quinbus Ninneter?" said Burton Topgallant. "I think we should know. What exactly is in there?"

◆

CHAPTER TWENTY-TWO

A NEW CHAPTER

It was a stack of old paper, as wrinkled as cloth, pages covered with a tight and faded handwriting. Michael read the first words aloud: "Travels Into Several Remote Nations of the World, by Captain Lemuel Gulliver." There was a date in the corner, 1725. Jane remembered the book, had spent time studying it at St. Brendan's.

Back in the old days, handwritten manuscripts were usually destroyed after a first publication, but here was the whole book and more. There was another section, never printed: "Part Five. A Voyage Back to Lilliput."

"I think," said Topgallant, "we need to know what's written here."

Michael and Jane settled in the wrecked village green, the brittle pages laid carefully before them. The Lesser Lilliputians found places to sit and listen, on benches, the ledges of shattered windows, in doorways, perched on broken rooftops.

And Michael began the new chapter . . .

CHAPTER I.

The Author's current situation described. A decision is reached. His much-loved ship, Adventure, is found after many long years. Some particulars of the voyage back to the Island.

AFTER MY RETURN from the land of the noble Houyhnhnm, I made every effort to reintegrate with Society. I vowed to my wife & children that I would wander no more.

In time, I took a position at the Royal Hospital of St. Brendan and enjoyed some success as a Surgeon. But, as weeks became months, the World seemed to grow stale around me. Compared to all I had seen, my own society was trivial & small. My comfortable home, I realized, was not the place I belonged.

I decided I would go where my voyage started, back to Lilliput. When my children reminded me of my vow to stay, I could only tell them that, "Promises & pie crusts were made to be broken." By chance, I found my beloved Adventure for sale in a local port, having been scuttled by its mutinous crew years before. She was filthy & tattered, but I recognized her figurehead immediately—the Mermaid, green eyes set on the future. I had the vessel re-fitted & employed a dependable crew & returned to the sea . . .

. . . With a map fresh in memory, I set a course for Lilliput. I will spare Readers details of the Voyage, except to say it was not easy. Pirates bedeviled us & we lay trapped for weeks in the Horse Latitudes. In the vast Indian Ocean, a monsoon nearly sank us.

On March 21st, 1724, we sighted that Blessed Isle, shimmering before us. We made anchor the next day, myself & a crew of 5 heading ashore by dinghy. How my heart raced! To be back, after so many years! As we entered harbor, I found the Port of Mildendo much changed in a quarter century. Buildings & shops were unpainted, unrepaired, walls pitted & pocked as if from gunfire.

I went to find my old friend, the Minister Reldresal. He was aged & frail, his eyesight having failed. He told me that among the younger generation, I had receded to Myth. Lilliputian Schoolchildren knew the legend of a Giant found lying in a field of clover, but none believed it.

Reldresal told me the Treaty with the Blefuscudians had broken & a bloody new war had raged for decades. I saw now that their Civilization was no better than my own . . .

. . . I was saddened, sickened, and wanted to leave right away. Several Lilliputians, also grown weary of war, wanted to return with me. But that was forbidden by the aged Emperor.

"I am honor-bound to respect your Nation's Laws," I told them.

Still, these small souls—among them, the Admiral of their Fleet—were desperate. "And if we followed on our ship?" the old sailor inquired. "Would you stop us?"

I had to admit, I could do nothing if they chose that course.

The next moonless night, they slipped aboard a ship in the harbor and seized control. Four dozen Lilliputians joined the bold escape, bringing horses, cows, sheep, geese, donkeys, chickens, pigs, children, older relatives and a few beloved pets. Leaving a lone guard bound and gagged on the dock, they set sail. Despite a superstition against it, they renamed their vessel Adventure, in homage to my own ship . . .

. . . I returned with them to Redriff & my family was delighted by the new houseguests. But others saw them as curiosities, suited for display in a Circus or Museum. We were besieged by gawking crowds. I quickly sold my house & purchased a small Farm outside Moss-on-Stone. I built a high Wall around the back garden & begged the Little Ones never to stray beyond it.

I let them imagine great Monsters & horrible Perils in the world outside. It was not easy to stand by as they dreamed up these awful things. But if it would keep them safe, I would let it happen.

They soon founded a New & Sovereign Nation and called it Lesser Lilliput. With the passing months & years, they seemed to forget their true home. They began to see me as a Giant in their world & no longer saw themselves as small things in my World.

Is it right that I should keep them hidden away? Will the Wall always be here to protect them? Or should I let them see the other World & learn who they really are?

CHAPTER TWENTY-THREE

◆

THE GHOSTS OF GIANTS

It was late-afternoon when he finished. Michael looked out on the sea of little faces and saw—what?—curiosity, fear. They wanted to know if the story was true. Did these pages tell their *real* story? As the first Lemuel Gulliver knew, they had long ago forgotten where they'd come from and who they were.

"Can it be . . . ?" Topgallant fumbled for words. "Is it possible . . . ? Are we *not* the only ones? Are we part of a larger race?"

"It sorta looks that way," said Michael.

In small huddled groups, the Lilliputians discussed this and all that it meant. To live so many years, thinking you were the only one of your kind and then to find you were part of some bigger thing . . .

Jane brushed the dusty bottom of the vault. "There's something else." It was a last sheet, a fading map. In the middle of a wide sea, just northwest of Van Diemen's Land, they saw the islands of Lilliput.

Now Michael knew what had to happen. "They're never going to be safe here, no matter what. I have to get them back. I have to get them home."

"How're we going to do that?" Jane asked.

"I think I know a way," he said. "You better let me handle it. You could get in a lot of trouble."

"I'm supposed to be grounded," said Jane, "but I helped break you out of prison. I'm a runaway. My picture's all over television. Unless you're planning on killing somebody, I couldn't get in much more trouble."

"Tomorrow, then," he said. "We'll get a good rest, and start tomorrow."

Michael used Lemuel's phone to call Charlie Ford and ask him to meet in the schoolyard, at dawn, and not tell a single soul.

Charlie had been there half an hour by the time Michael made his way through alleys and back gardens. "I need you to buy me something."

"I saw you on the news, Michael," Charlie sniffled. "You and a girl, they say you're missing. Are you, Michael?"

"I'm here talking to you, so I'm not too missing," he answered. "But that's why I need you. I have to keep out of sight for a while. Will you help me, Charlie?"

The littler boy thought about it and said, "I could end up on TV, too."

"Yeah," said Michael. He wasn't going to lie. "You really could, Charlie."

"That'd be wicked cool." Charlie wiped his runny nose.

"Will you help?" Michael asked. "It's not going to be easy."

"Why'd you ask *me*, Michael?" Charlie wanted to know. "You could've asked Penelope Rees or somebody smart."

"Penelope knows stuff, but she isn't smart. She couldn't help, but I know you can do it, Charlie."

He thought for a moment and said, "I'll help, Michael, if you tell me what's going on. All of it."

And Michael told him. He told the whole story: Lemuel and the Lilliputians, the fire in the Garden City, YOI, Jane, all of it.

"All right," Charlie said when he finished, "that's all I wanted to know. I'll help you. Just tell me what to do."

"That's not nearly enough money," Gadbury told Charlie. "You got, what, fourteen, fifteen pounds here. Another twenty in trade for this bike. You got, say, a total of thirty-five pounds here. That thing's worth a hundred fifty, easy."

"No, it's not," the boy sniffled as he looked over the ship model. "It's in lousy shape. You'd have to spend another hundred just to get it fixed."

"It's old," Gadbury said.

"It's falling apart," Charlie said back.

"I could get ninety for it and you know it."

And Charlie did know it. "I have a fifty pound note in my shoe," he said.

"Sure you do," Gadbury laughed.

"My nan gave it to me." Charlie took out the note and smoothed it on the counter. "Altogether that makes eighty-five."

"Allrightyeahallright," Gadbury grumbled and took the money.

"I need a way to get it back," Charlie added. "You can throw in that wagon over there."

"And all for eighty-five pounds! Are you trying to rob me?!"

"I'm in a hurry, bud," Charlie sniffed.

"You little runny-nosed brass neck!" But Gadbury helped load the old ship model. "This thing weighs more than you do, kid." It was as big as a sofa and barely balanced in the wagon, but Charlie set off down the street with it.

Michael waited, by a hedge, at the edge of town. He saw police cars cruising the narrow streets, looking for him, looking for Jane. As he waited, a new wind began to blow across Moss-on-Stone and in it you could smell the sea.

A little after ten, he saw Charlie struggling with the wagon and the big model ship. "Thanks, Charlie. I really owe you."

"No," said Charlie. "You really don't." And he left.

It took a full hour to get the wagon back to the stone cottage. The Little Ones set to work refitting it, caulking its hull, stocking its larder.

Michael and Jane went to the cottage and started searching through boxes. Inside, everything was perfect and still and windless. "Here's one," Michael called when he found a map of the county. "It's old, but roads don't change. It'll do, right?"

Jane unfolded the map on a table. "Yeah, look, there," she pointed. "There's a canal, here, just outside Ambridge. It leads to the river."

"That's what we need," said Michael.

But Jane shook her head. "It's fifteen miles, Michael. And we have to carry that big ship and all the people. How can we even dream of doing something like that?"

CHAPTER TWENTY-FOUR

---- ◆ ----

THE ALL-NEW 1926 HISPANO-SUIZA

I think I know a way."

He took the old key and went to the barn, not really sure what he'd find. They got the rotting door open and saw a wood crate—eight feet high, sixteen feet long, marked for delivery to Lemuel Gulliver.

"It's from France, Bois-Colombes," Jane read the marking.

They found hammers and prying bars and went at it. Each aged nail screamed as it was pulled from the wood. They peeled back the first panel and, under a blanket of dust and smoky web, they saw a giant motorcar. When they cut the steel straps that still held it, gravity rolled the monster into the farmyard.

A crowd of Little Ones stood watching a custom-built 1926 Hispano-Suiza move into sunlight, fourteen feet long, spoked-wood wheels, a canvas top folded open. The dashboard was ivory and rosewood, seats a dark leather, the carpet thick and wool. There were flower vases by the rear seats, still with the ghost-stems of roses.

"Looks like it's never been used," said Jane.

"I don't think he even opened the crate," Michael told her.

"Do you figure it'll still run?"

Philament Phlopp had already crawled into the engine. "I can make it work," he said. "We'll need some petrol, oil, an hour or two."

"But even if you got it running," said Jane, "*who* would drive it?"

"I will," Michael answered. He'd driven a digital Formula One racing car and how much harder could this be? If his feet could reach the pedals, he could drive it. He wiped greasy dust from the ornament. "It's a stork." A silver stork in flight was the Hispano-Suiza's emblem. "They're good luck, y'know."

Mr. Phlopp spent an hour and a half inside the engine, clearing lines, cleaning each of the eight cylinders. He had everything working perfectly, except the canvas top: the metal ribs had frozen in place and would have to stay down.

Michael and Jane and the Little Ones brought the heavy ship model around and tied it across a grille on the back. It overhung the car by a few feet.

Everything was near-ready now and Topgallant organized the Exodus. Standing on the toppled town fountain, he called for the others to, "Gather livestock, pets, children, older relatives. Hurry, and bring only the essentials!"

They moved quickly, wrapping hopes and dreams in tablecloths and leaving the rest behind. Soon, a hundred ninety-one Lilliputians were gathering by the barn, ready to board their rolling ark. Burton Topgallant had a list and saw that every name was accounted for . . . all but two.

Brave Mr. Wellup had been lost to the weasels and Hoggish Butz was nowhere to be found.

After a quick search of the wrecked city, Topgallant saw him outside the trampled bakery, calmly chewing a stale éclair, Golden Helmet glinting in the mid-morning sun. "It's time, Brother Butz," said Burton. "We have to get moving."

"We are *NOT* going," Hoggish hmphed at him. "I am the Grand Panjandrum and *I* say we *STAY*. It is my decree, it is law."

Burton Topgallant looked over the ruined city and sighed, "There's no one left to listen, Brother Butz."

Hoggish only straightened the Gold Helmet and sniffed, "This is my kingdom. It is my *HOME*."

"It was a home for us all, once." Topgallant took a seat across from him. "But it isn't anymore. We're part of a greater race, you and me and the rest, and we need to join it."

Hoggish was silent and still.

"Besides, if you stay here—what will you eat?"

"Oh, Great Ghost of Bolgolam . . . ," sighed Mr. Butz.

The Lesser Lilliputians loaded into the car, all of them and with room to spare: it was even more massive than their Great Hall had been.

"Wait, hold on," said Jane.

"What for?" asked Michael.

"We can't drive it like this."

"Why not?" the boy wanted to know.

"Look at it," she said. "It's a mess."

And it was, covered with decades of dust that dulled its paint and chrome. "We should clean it," she said. "We should make it look nice."

But Michael shook his head. "There isn't time."

"It won't take LONG." Hoggish had quietly joined them.

They agreed it was something they owed Quinbus Flestrin and, with soap and water and little rags, they went at it. The Lesser Lilliputians were all over the car, scrubbing every hidden inch. Wool carpets were cleaned, leather oiled, ivory and rosewood polished, new flowers found for the vases. Within an hour, the Hispano-Suiza shined as it had on a day in 1926.

"All right," said Jane. "Let's go."

Michael started the huge engine and it hummed, healthy and full of life. He told everyone to hold on as he made a wide long turn in the field and drove up the rutted gravel road, out onto the single carriageway.

There were no cars, no lorries, no tractors on the main road. A sudden warm wind swept in from behind them and Jane's hair flew wild and free.

"Clap on full sail," called Topgallant. "We're riding with the wind."

The old car pulled from the farm, for the first and last time, and headed toward an unseen sea.

When Stanley Ford came by a few hours later, searching for Michael Pine and Jane Mallery, he would find the stone cottage quiet and empty and still. In the back, by the barn, he would find a pile of tiny wet rags.

If you've ever been twelve years old and at the wheel of an Hispano-Suiza, top down, throttle out, you know it's a powerful feeling—the road, hills, and patchwork farms sailing past, the miles melting beneath you.

Jane folded the road map in her lap and watched the fields of mop-headed cows and long-fleeced sheep go by. The Lesser Lilliputians peered out at a world they'd never Imagined, never Dreamed was here.

Michael eased the long car through a roundabout. As they drove through a small village, the road narrowed to pass between a church and an inn, and he misjudged the turn. The old car bounced hard on a stone curb, shaking, rattling to its frame. The big ship model nearly fell from the back grille.

"Is everything all right, you think?" Jane asked.

"Don't know," Michael answered, but everything wasn't. A rear tire was punctured and going flat.

"I think the children may have been at the Gulliver cottage," Officer Ford phoned to tell Horace Ackerby. "Somebody's been here, anyway. Within the last few hours, I'd say."

This time, the Magistrate himself called for the APW.

There was a petrol station and restaurant at the far edge of this village and Michael pulled the car to a stop. The children got out and saw a very flat tire. "Is there another one?" Jane asked. "A spare?"

"If there is," said Michael, "I wouldn't know how to put it on."

Thudd Ickens slipped out of the car and crawled across the tire. "It's only a small puncture, on the inside, close to the rim. Nothing too bad."

"You think these people can fix it here, at the station?" Jane asked. "I have a little money, not much."

"Maybe," said Michael and he headed to the service bay.

"What you want?" came a voice.

Michael hadn't seen the mechanic, half under a car. "We— my Dad— we have a flat tire. Can you fix it?" the boy asked.

"Not now I can't," came the voice. "Give me a half hour."

"All right," said Michael, "thanks." But he didn't have a half hour to give. When he saw a patch kit on the work-bench, he grabbed it and hurried out.

Philament Phlopp was sure that he and Ickens could repair the tire. They took the patch and climbed back to find the puncture. Michael knelt and tried to help them, but a man in tweed was walking toward them from the station's restaurant. "Michael, somebody's coming," Jane whispered. She quietly called for the Lesser Lilliputians to hide themselves.

"There's something you don't see every day," the tweedy man was saying and he meant the car. "What is it, '28, '29?"

" '26," Michael answered.

"It's remarkable," the man went on. "Think it might be for sale?"

"No," Jane told him. "My Dad loves this car."

"I can see why," the man said, looking over the Hispano-Suiza. "Looks like it's never been used, like it was just made." The children said nothing. "I'd like to talk to your Dad about it."

"Okay," said Michael and he moved to block the view of the rear seat.

"Where is he?" the man wanted to know.

"He's. Inside. In there," Jane pointed to the restaurant. "In the lavatory, I think."

The man in tweed nodded and said, "Yeah, maybe I'll ask him about it."

A moment after he left, Phlopp called that the tire was patched. "You can fill it again," Ickens said as Jane helped them into the car. Michael was adding air to the tire when the mechanic called to him from the service bay. "Tell your Dad I'm about ready. I'll patch that tire in a minute."

"*We have to go,*" Jane whispered and grabbed the road map and went to stall the mechanic.

Michael kept filling the tire, checking that the patch was holding.

"We're a little lost," Jane told the mechanic in the bay, stalling, spreading the old map on the workbench. "Can you show us how to get to Ambridge?"

A half-minute later, Michael had the tire filled and the car started. "Jane," he called out. The man in tweed was coming from the restaurant. "Jane, let's go!"

"Hey, kids," called the man. "I can't find your father in there."

Jane ran from the bay and jumped in the car and they sped away, leaving the mechanic and tweedy man to wonder.

They headed out of the little town, past a bronze statue of St. George and his Dragon. They were a mile down the road when Jane remembered, "The map, Michael, the map to Ambridge, I left it in the station!"

"I know the way," he said. "I was locked up there, remember?"

"But the river, can you find that? We have to find the river to reach the sea."

Burton Topgallant happened to look up and happened to see two great birds, broad-winged, long-beaked, flying together far overhead. "Look there!" he cried. "Mr. Gulliver's storks are coming home."

Michael saw the giant birds and knew they'd flown from Africa, from over the ocean. He watched their path, south to north, toward the next rolling mountain. "We need to go where they came from," he told Jane. "Then we'll find the sea."

The road lifted into a forest and small birds watched from telephone wires and the sun moved lower on the horizon.

"Brother Ninneter . . ." Topgallant popped his head over the front seat. "Bit of a problem." Michael and Jane saw a police car following on the rising, falling road.

"Maybe they aren't looking for us," said Michael, turning at a roundabout to keep going south.

But the police car turned, too, and followed.

"They are," said Jane. "They are, Michael."

There was a tractor ahead and he slowed to pass. "We have to get to Ambridge," he said. "One way or other, we have to get them home."

Jane held the door handle tight and said, "See how fast it can go, Michael."

He pushed the pedal to the floor and Burton Topgallant went flying into the backseat. The old motor was awake now and remembering just how fast it could go—80, 85, 90 miles per hour. The faster it went, the more sure of the road it became. Farmland streamed by like rain from a cloud.

The police tried to keep up, but the Hispano-Suiza was too much car. As he left the cops behind, Michael began to think they might make it after all.

But it wasn't long until they saw more police ahead, coming toward them from the north, east and west, a dozen sets of flashing lights speeding at them. The road was blocked and Michael had to let the big car slow.

"Hold on," he said, jerking through an open farm gate. He took the car across a field of fresh-plowed wheat. The Hispano-Suiza bounced over deep ruts and Lesser Lilliputians flew like kernels of popping corn.

The police cars tried following, but couldn't manage the rough field. The old car rode high and over the furrows, but all the dozen police were soon stuck fast in the dirt.

Michael drove over one field and through the next, until a stone wall stopped them. The town of Ambridge was just beyond. The car stopped with a sudden lurch and a shudder, its motor dead. Michael found an old wheelbarrow and they piled the giant ship model in. The Lesser Lilliputians walked as fast as their small legs let them and they set off, leaving the car behind in the field.

Night was falling as they reached the village, its streets full of music and dancers, a fair, a festival, like they used to have in Moss-on-Stone. Michael and Jane found a wrecked rusted shopping cart and loaded most of the Lesser Lilliputians into it, covering them with an old sheet. The rest rode in the wheelbarrow with the ship model.

There were police officers everywhere, but the children lost themselves in the celebration—a talent of Michael's—and the cops never saw them. The smell of warm food was almost too much for the Little Ones; still they listened to Jane and stayed out of view.

Down a block more, Jane saw the canal sparkling with moonlight. They found the place where the longboats were docked for the night and Michael went to the closed rental office. Once, these narrow boats had carried merchandise up and down the small canals that connected the country; now they carried only tourists. Michael read the trip rates: five pounds for an hour, fifteen for half a day, thirty for the full.

"I don't have that much," Jane told him quietly.

But he wasn't worried. "You wait here," he said to her. "I'll take care of it." There was a small gift shop by the longboats, also closed for the night, and Jane huddled the Lesser Lilliputians under its wide sheltering eaves.

Michael went back to the village, wandering its crowded streets until he found the old coin shop he remembered from another day. It was shut, locked, but lights still glowed from a second floor room where the owner lived. The boy hammered the door with his fists, rattling the door on its hinges, until the bald young man came to open it.

"I'm closed, come back in the morning."

But Michael put his arm in the door before the man could shut it. "I'm sorry, but I need—"

"Go away or I'll call the police!"

"Can you tell me what this is worth?" And he opened his hand and held out the coin Lem had given him, that first day at Fenn's market.

When the dealer saw it, he let the boy in and locked the store tight behind them. "Where'd you get this?"

"It was given to me," Michael told him. "Is it worth something?"

The young coin dealer nodded. "This is from India, kid, an 1841 Mohur," he said, looking at it through his glass. "Lion and palm, with the error here, on Victoria. The cast is off-center. There, you see? Didn't you ever look at it twice? A small dent on the reverse, otherwise perfect. This coin is worth two thousands pounds, easily. With the right collectors bidding, it might go for three times that."

"Would you buy it?" asked Michael.

"Kid, I don't have that kind of money. You need to get this to a city and a good auction house."

"You can have it for fifty pounds," the boy said.

But the dealer gave him back the coin. "I won't do that. This thing could be worth a hundred times more."

Michael set it on the counter. "All I need is fifty."

The young man shook his head, saying, "No, no, no," again and again.

Michael begged, "It's really important. I don't care what it's worth. All I need is fifty pounds. You can have it for fifty."

The dealer kept shaking his head, even as he unlocked the cash drawer in his dark oaken desk. "Here," he sighed, "this is a down payment, and that's all it is. You come back, kid, and we'll sell the coin together."

Michael thanked him and went.

As he hurried back to the canal, he passed a dim, dingy pub where a stubbly-faced man sat smoking and drinking by the front window. The man looked up and saw the little boy through the haze and knew him.

"Hold on now," the taxi driver said to himself.

Michael went into the village fair to find food. He walked the loud, busy streets, past a volunteer band and a troupe of morris dancers, kid-rides, vendors in tents, the whole place crazy with sound and light. He wished his own village were like this, full of music, full of life. He stopped at the street stalls and filled three sacks with food.

Back by the river, he emptied the bags and they all had a feast of fish cakes and pizza fingers, sausages and pasties.

The Lesser Lilliputians were humbled and grateful for all the boy had done to help them. "I don't see how we'll repay you for this," said Topgallant.

"As soon as it's light," Michael told him, "we'll finish the journey."

But even as he said this, a man was stumbling down the dock toward them, with a hollow thumping of planks. The Little Ones hid, quickly, expertly. Michael and Jane couldn't see who it was in the dark.

"Knew that was you." The stubble-faced man stepped into a pool of moonlight. "The two little runaways." It was the taxi driver.

Jane and Michael were stuck where they were and had nowhere to run: there was only one way off the dock and the man stood blocking it.

"We don't want any trouble," Michael told him. "Just get away from us."

"Tough kid," the driver laughed. "What're you, ten?"

"Twelve," said Michael. "How much do you want to go away?"

"Ha. More'n you got," the man said, slurred.

"Would you go and forget you saw us . . . for fifty pounds?"

"Like y'got that," he laughed.

Michael pulled out the notes and showed him. "Here. Take it. All we want is to be left alone."

"For fifty pounds, might jus' do that."

Michael held out the money and said, "Now go."

The stubbly man laughed and said nothing more, but grabbed the money and left them, stumbling and fumbling and mumbling back up the dock. They watched till darkness took him. "He might still turn us in," said Jane. "He might take the money and still go to the cops."

"Not him," Michael told her. "He's like Freddie. He'll go back to the pub."

And the man did. He went back to the pub and didn't leave till it closed. By then, he'd forgotten all about the children.

"Now we don't have any money," said Jane. "Where do we go from here?"

——— ✦ ———

CHAPTER TWENTY-FIVE

THE LONGBOAT

That coin was worth a lot," Michael told her and showed her another wad of money. "The man in the shop gave me a hundred for it and said there'd be more. We still have enough."

They settled under the eaves and they slept.

The sun rose slowly that next dawn and the canal mist didn't burn away. A family of moorhen pattered to the water and a trout gulped a meal from the once-still surface. Over where the longboats were docked, Jane woke to see the booking agent opening his stall. She nudged Michael. "C'mon," she whispered. "It's time."

Jane went to the clerk, who was getting his forms ready, and asked about renting a boat.

"Five pounds for an hour," he said.

"Okay," she said and, "we'll take a full day," and she put thirty pounds on the counter.

The man looked up from his work. "And where would Mum and Dad be, love?"

"They're divorced," she said as she opened her rucksack behind her back, and Thudd Ickens slipped out. "My Dad's over there," and she waved, that-way-somewhere.

The booking agent stepped around his stand and began setting out a large signboard and Ickens ran off, unseen, the other way.

"He sent me with the money," Jane said and showed him the notes again. "Thirty pounds. It's all here. We want to rent a boat for the whole day."

"That's good, that's fine. But I'm not going to rent to a little girl, am I?"

"Why not?" She was stalling now, giving Ickens time to grab the key.

"It's against what we call the law, love."

"But I have the money, see? Right here." She picked up the notes and waved them once again. "Thirty pounds."

The little acrobat was shimmying up an electric wire, tightroping across a coat-rack to reach the box that held the boat keys.

"Yes, love, I saw," said the agent. "But I still need a real grown-up with real grown-up identification, y'understand?"

Jane saw Thudd Ickens, the key slung over his shoulder, as he crawled into the rucksack. "Well, okay. I'll get Dad then," she told the agent.

"Yeah, you do that."

She left the money on the counter and ran away.

"Hold on—! Don't leave this here—! Hey—!"

But she was gone.

"Kids," the man sighed to himself.

A hundred feet away, at the water's edge, Michael found the longboat to match the key number. The agent had wandered up to the village, for coffee. Jane kept watch as Michael hurried the Lesser Lilliputians aboard, all one hundred ninety-two of them. Last of all, they loaded the giant ship model onto the stern.

Another minute later, Michael had the motor running and Jane untied the lines. They drifted into the canal, clumsily banging other boats, as she stood at the bow and called directions.

The booking clerk was still gone and didn't see, but a lone fisherman, with a long Buddha gaze, watched from the opposite embankment. Jane smiled and waved shyly as they hit a few more boats.

The fisherman nodded. "Everything all right over there?"

"My Dad," said Jane, "he's— he's not so great with boats."

"There are bigger sins than that," the fisherman said.

At last they were clear, in the middle of the waterway, and on their awkward way. The longboat cruised drunkenly down the old canal, sideswiping pilings and trees. Jane and the Lilliputians held on tight. "Michael, is this the best you can do?"

"I never drove one of these," was the answer from the cabin.

Jane had to look away when they nearly ran down a Snow Goose. A willow drooped to the water and the reeds were overgrown and the longboat plowed on through it all. Soon, Michael got them back in open water and they picked up speed.

It wasn't long before Jane saw another canal boat ahead, loaded with early-morning sightseers, its captain eyeing the boat headed toward him at a dangerous clip.

"Watch your course!" came his far-off call. "Easy, easy there!"

"To your left, Michael, your left!" Jane called.

The longboat turned straight for the other boat, full-speed.

"Hove her to, man! Now, now!"

"Your *other* left!" Jane called to Michael and at the last impossible second, he steered them away—too late for a clean pass—and they went crunching down the side of the tour boat, two hulls crying out as the wood rubbed together. "Sorry," Jane said as they passed, and again, "sorry."

The tour captain was furious, trying to kick the other boat clear. "Who's your captain?!"

Jane shrugged and shyly said, "My Dad."

"Let me see him, now!"

Michael only pushed the engine harder, speeding away. But as they passed, the tour captain got a glimpse of the young boy at the helm.

And he grabbed for the wireless.

Twenty minutes later, they heard a siren. It was the Marine Patrol now, steering an expert course around and between other boats on the river. The children saw two policemen in it, and a large dark figure besides. Michael knew it was Horace Ackerby, Chief Magistrate for Moss-on-Stone. There was no mistaking that giant.

The river here felt the ocean tide, and it was going out fast. The longboat was flying along, pushed by its engine and pulled by the ebbing sea. But the Marine Patrol was moving quickly, too, closer and closer.

"They're coming, Michael. They're going to catch us."

The boy could see the other officer, Stanley Ford. When the call had first come in from the tour captain, that the children had been seen in the river near Ambridge, he and the Magistrate had left immediately.

"Don't let them get away from us," said Ackerby.

"Not a chance," the pilot told him.

◆ ◆ ◆ ◆ ◆

Michael tried to coax the longboat faster, but the engine had no more to give. He wasn't watching the quick-dropping water and ran onto a sandbar. There was loud grinding and they were all thrown from their feet, Michael, Jane, the Lesser Lilliputians.

"What was that?" cried Jane.

"Don't know," Michael said, gunning the engine again and again. But the longboat was stuck tight in the mud.

"Looks like the end of your journey," the officer called to Michael.

But the boy knew it wasn't. Deep in his pocket was a crumbled and singed piece of paper: *No journey has an end*, it said. The Marine Patrol thumped the longboat's stern.

"I'm really sorry," Michael quietly told Jane, "for getting you into this mess."

"Don't be," she told him. "It was fun."

Stanley Ford was helping the children onto the police cruiser when the Magistrate saw something downriver. "Wait a minute," he said. "What's that thing?"

"What's what thing, sir?" Ford asked.

"There, out in the river." He pointed and the other officers looked. "What *is* it?"

Far down the broad river, a ship the size of a sofa was sailing away, all sails unfurled.

"Looks like a model," the pilot said. "A kid's toy."

"Is it yours?" Stanley asked the children.

"No," Michael answered.

"I know what that is." The Magistrate—like Cicero, a seeker of Truth—reached for the binoculars in the cruiser cabin. "It's the old wood ship that's been in the window at Gadbury's since I was a child."

The Magistrate scanned the river till he found the *Adventure's* bow, and a tiny carved mermaid, eyes set on the future. A small tattered flag still hung from the spar. Michael had wanted to take it off; it was old and worn. "Let's leave it," Mrs. Topgallant had said to him. "It's the flag that's flown when the Admiral of the Fleet is on board."

"Did you steal that thing?" Stanley asked Michael.

"No—we bought it."

"Must've cost a lot," said the officer.

"I guess," Michael nodded. "But it was worth it."

"Are you telling me," Stanley went on, "you spent all that money, just so you could let it go in the river?"

"That's right," Jane answered.

The Magistrate brought the little ship into better focus and saw the crew of tiny People, swarming its rigging, tightening the sails. On its deck, a crowd of tiny passengers gathered at the rail, watching the passing scene. And he saw another man looking straight back at him through a little telescope: Burton Topgallant, former G.P., Potentate, Pooh-Bah, Keeper of Hopes, the End-All, Be-All, and Admiral of the Fleet. Topgallant lowered the glass and saluted Ackerby.

"Sir?" Stanley was saying now.

"What?" the Magistrate mumbled, fumbled.

"Do we need it for evidence?"

"Need what?" Horace was struck half-dumb by what he'd seen.

"The model. The little ship. If we need it for evidence, we can get it."

"No," the Magistrate answered finally. "No. Let it go."

Ford looked to the children. "And what about them? What'll we charge 'em with?"

CHAPTER TWENTY-SIX

◆

BACK IN A FIELD OF CLOVER

Stanley Ford had already begun filling out the paperwork. "Sir . . . ," he said again, trying to get the Magistrate's attention back.

"What?"

"The children," Ford reminded him. "What's the charge going to be?"

"The children. Yes," said Ackerby. "Let the children go."

"Let them what?" Stanley hadn't heard him right. "Let them go? Mr. Ackerby, they took a boat and there was the car and—"

"I'll take care of it," the Magistrate said.

The officers were confused, and so was Michael.

"But the boy," Stanley went on, "he broke out of YOI, remember."

"I remember," the Magistrate said. "I'll take care of it." And that's all he would say.

Adventure sailed on down the mud-brown river, past a spreading city where the water was full of cargo vessels and barges and broad-hulled tour boats. Anyone who saw the model ship took it for a lost toy.

The Lesser Lilliputians stood at the rail and marveled at this race of Giants and all they'd achieved: the dome of a great cathedral here, the towers of a bridge there, an ancient seat of government.

The sea-tide was pulling them at a fast clip and the river grew more crowded. Burton Topgallant called out commands, steering them clear of heavy water traffic. "To the port, steady! Trim the aft sails!" He'd only read the words in books, but now they had meaning.

And their ship sailed on.

"Do you suppose they'll get along without us?" Docksey asked her husband. "The children? They're so young and vulnerable."

"They're more capable than you'd think, my dear," said Topgallant. "You must remember, vulnerable creatures have ways of getting by."

Adventure reached a wide channel and the sea lay beyond.

◆ ◆ ◆ ◆ ◆

When Michael and Jane got home, Ackerby told Jane's father what had happened, almost every detail. There were television cameras waiting, but Ms. Bellknap said the children had been through a lot and needed to be left alone. Mr. Mallery took a second, longer look at Michael and liked what he saw.

And at the same moment, something happened that has never been explained. By some unimaginable shift in climate, the raw ugly wind suddenly stopped blowing across Moss-on-Stone. For the first time ever, the sun shone a whole day and there was only the softest breeze in the treetops. From that day and ever after, the city was known as *Moss-on-Stone, Where No Wind's Blown*.

In the warming sun, as Maxine Bellknap immediately saw, the seed of chickweed and dandelion—favorite foods of House Sparrows—took root everywhere and began to thrive.

An envelope arrived at the Magistrate's office not long after. It held a deed and a stack of legal papers, giving Michael the stone cottage and all that was in it. Freddie was carefully, legally, left out.

Over time, the Lesser Lilliputians drifted into legend. People from around the world have heard the story of Little Ones who wander the clover fields here. Hordes of visitors still come seeking them and tour buses stop in the town and the Inn is booked months in advance.

In the years since, Michael and Jane have repaired the damage done to Lesser Lilliput. They have restored every structure, replanted the tiny gardens, rebuilt the Great Hall and its glorious dome. You can go there and see this yourself, if you know where to look.

And when you're in Moss-on-Stone, listen closely. In the stillness, you may hear Mr. Fenn trying to wheedle a tune from his ancient guitar. Just this morning, he picked up the phone and called an old friend: "I've been thinking— we should get the band together. Yes, The Restless Ones, you remember. You, me, Froth, Gadbury, Larry Tiswas, the rest— making music like we used to. How about it, Horace?"

FROM THE DIARY OF YOUNG
FRIGARY TIDDLIN

A Friday, late in September—

We are home and a new journey begins. Slack & I have made many friends in school & Mr. Topgallant is writing a chronicle of our lives in the other world.

Mr. Ickens has become a Popular Lecturer and Mr. Phlopp's eyebrows are starting to grow back. The brothers Butz are quiet & sullen, but I'm sure they'll come to love this place. Life is good again, because we found something we never knew we'd Lost.

But we'd lost it, that's for sure. Back in that other Time & Place, we thought we understood everything. We didn't Know how much we didn't Know. Now we do, and we have begun to Dream again . . .

So, nat'ralists observe, a flea
Hath smaller fleas that on him prey
And these have smaller yet to bite 'em,
And so proceed ad infinitum . . .
Thus ev'ry poet, in his kind,
Is bit by him that comes behind.

On Poetry, Jonathan Swift